The Adventure of the Engineer's Mom

A New Sherlock Holmes Mystery

Note to Readers:

Your enjoyment of this new Sherlock Holmes mystery will be enhanced by re-reading the original story that inspired this one –

The Adventure of the Engineer's Thumb.

It has been appended and may be found in the back portion of this book.

THE ADVENTURE OF THE ENGINEER'S MOM

CRAIG STEPHEN COPLAND

The Adventure of the Engineer's Mom

A New Sherlock Holmes Mystery #11

Craig Stephen Copland

Published by:

Conservative Growth Inc.
3104 30th Avenue, Suite 427
Vernon, British Columbia, Canada
V1T 9M9

Cover design by Rita Toews.

ISBN 10: 1514341689

ISBN 13: 978-1514341681

Dedication

To research scientists throughout the world, most of whom will never be famous but who will devote their lives, hard work, and brilliant minds to trying to make this world better for all of us.

.

Welcome to New Sherlock Holmes Mysteries –

"The best-selling series of new Sherlock Holmes stories. All faithful to The Canon."

Each story is a tribute to one of the sixty original stories about the world's most famous detective. If you are encountering these new stories for the first time, start with *Studying Scarlet,* and keep going. (https://www.amazon.com/dp/B07CW3C9YZ)

If you subscribe to Kindle Unlimited, then you can 'borrow for free' every one of the books.

They are all available as ebooks, paperbacks, hardcovers, and in large print.

Check them out at www.SherlockHolmesMysteries.com.

NEW SHERLOCK HOLMES MYSTERIES

WWW.SHERLOCKHOLMESMYSTERY.COM

THE RETURN OF NAPOLEON

The Adventure of Mata Hari's Harem

THE ADVENTURE OF THE NORWOOD REMBRANDT

THE SOLITARY BICYCLE THIEF

THE ADVENTURE OF MRS. J. H. HELLER

THE ADVENTURE OF THE PRIORESS'S TALE

THE DANCER FROM THE DANCE

THE MYSTERY OF THE FIVE ORANGES

THE GLORIOUS YACHT

THE GRECIAN EARNED

THE HIDDEN VALLEY MYSTERY

A CASE OF IDENTITY THEFT

THE IMPATIENT DISSIDENTS

A MOST GRAVE RITUAL

THE NAVAL KNAVES

STUDYING SCARLET

THE ADVENTURE OF THE SECOND STIPEND

THE SILVER HORSE, BRAISED

THE SPY GATE GIRLS

THE STOCK MARKET MURDERS

THE THREE ROBBO'S NOT TAKEN

THE ADVENTURE OF THE MISSING BETTER HALF

THE INEQUALITY OF MERCY

THE MAN WHO WAS TWISTED BUT HIP

THE YELLOW FARCE

THE MYSTERY OF 222 BAKER STREET

THE ADVENTURE OF THE SPECTRED HAT

THE ADVENTURE OF THE BLUE BELT BUCKLE

THE ADVENTURE OF THE DEVILISH FOOTNOTE

THE ADVENTURE OF THE BERYL ANARCHISTS

THE BOX OF CARDS

THE BALD-HEADED TRUST

THE ADVENTURE OF THE MORNING GLORY MURDERS

THE BINOMIAL ASTEROID PROBLEM

THE VILLAGE

THE DYING DEBUTANTE

THE KIDNAPPING OF BABY CARLAX

ADVENTURE OF THE INSANE MILITANO

THE ADVENTURE OF THE DEVILISH FOOTNOTE

THE SIGN OF THE TOOTH

CRAIG STEPHEN COPLAND

Contents

Acknowledgments

All writers of pastiche stories of Sherlock Holmes must acknowledge their debt to Sir Arthur Conan Doyle and to the Sacred Canon of the original stories. Or, if you are a hopeless Sherlockian, then to Dr. John H. Watson, who wrote almost all of the stories and that Doyle chap who was his literary agent and got *The Strand* to publish them.

I discovered *The Adventures of Sherlock Holmes* while a student at Scarlett Heights Collegiate Institute in Toronto. My English teachers – Bill Stratton, Norm Oliver, and Margaret Tough – inspired me to read and write. I shall be forever grateful to them.

The plot and characters of this novella are inspired by and adapted freely from *The Adventure of the Engineer's Thumb*. The new and original mystery story was greatly aided, as are all of my stories, by Google and Wikipedia.

My dearest and best friend, Mary Engelking, read all drafts, helped with whatever historical and geographical accuracy was required, and offered insightful recommendations for changes to the narrative structure, characters, and dialogue. Thank you.

Many words and whole phrases and sentences have been lifted and copied shamelessly and joyfully from the sacred canon of Sherlockian literature. Should any word or turn of phrase strike the reader as the *mot juste,* you may count on its having been plagiarized.

For the very idea of writing a new Sherlock Holmes mystery, I thank the Bootmakers, the Sherlock Holmes Society of Canada.

Chapter One

The Wounded Engineer

The contrast between the pleasant serenity of the locale of my new medical practice and the strange and brutal events of the case that began, there could not be more stark and unforgettable. It was only the second case that I had introduced to the notice of my friend and former roommate, Sherlock Holmes, and although it began as no more than a concern for finding an aging parent, it escalated into one of international intrigue, greed, guile, and murder. There have been several brief accounts in the press, all incomplete and misleading. It is useful, therefore, to place the details of the case, *The Adventure of the Engineer's Mom,* now upon record *en bloc* so that the citizens of Britain, the Empire, and those other countries who follow the adventures of Sherlock Holmes may have a full understanding of how he put his unique powers of imagination and deduction to work in bringing a solution to this mystery.

The year of Our Lord 1899 brought England the coldest summer in living memory. Some of the scientists down in Greenwich were claiming that the frigid weather was caused by all of the coal gas and dust our factories were belching into the atmosphere and blocking out the sunlight. They were prophesying that if we did not mend our ways, the next ice age would soon be upon us. Others said that it was no more than a passing instance wrought by the massive explosion of the Krakatoa volcano on the other side of the globe and that it was only a hiccup in Nature's grand scheme and would soon pass. Regardless, the weather had been miserable, even for England.

I had recently opened a surgery just north of Paddington Station and within sight of that part of England's Grand Canal that had been dubbed our Little Venice. The poet who gave it that name, the one the wags called Alfie Tennis Anyone, can be forgiven his pretensions and exaggeration since this quiet corner of our great metropolis had long ceased to be an industrial harbor. It had become a garden of delight where ladies and gentlemen and families with children went to enjoy the view of the small lake and the sounds of the abundant bird life. The greatest disturbance was likely to be no more than a barking dog or a screeching infant.

What had begun as a mere trickle of patients to my surgery had turned into a steady flow. I had advertised at Paddington Station amongst the railway employees, and a growing number of them had found it convenient to drop in to see me once their shifts had ended. Most of them had nothing wrong with them that a prescription of one or two good nights' sleep would not cure, yet they swore by my healing abilities when their symptoms vanished and proceeded to refer their railway colleagues and passengers to me. One chap, Terrance Fitzmorris, had a dreadful and embarrassing cough that he feared was caused by tuberculosis and was certain that he was not only going to die but that before doing so, he would be let go from the Great Western for fear of infecting the passengers. I had cured him by giving him a bottle of sugar pills, tainted with a few drops of alum so as to make them taste like a respectable medicine. I had told him, however, that the pills would not only fail to cure him but would make matters worse if their essences came into contact with tobacco smoke. On pain of death, he immediately ceased using his cigarettes, and within three weeks, his cough had vanished. He became my most loyal reference.

And so it was on a Thursday in late July that at half-past five o'clock, just past sunrise, I was up and ready to take myself for my chilly morning walk along the canal when there came a knock to my door. I opened it to see Terry, looking hale and hearty, but with his arm around a young man, not more than five and twenty, who was obviously in debilitating pain.

"Good morning, Doctor Watson," said Terry. "Knew you would be up and at 'em already so I just had to bring this lad to see you. He's in a bit of a rough shape he is. Aren't you there, laddie?"

The poor fellow said nothing but nodded. Even though it was a crisp morning, the sweat was dripping off of his face, and he was struggling to breathe. A deadly dizziness appeared to have come over him, so I motioned for Terry to enter help the lad into my examining room. He pulled one of the fellow's arms over his shoulders and put his own strong arm around the waist and started walking. The young fellow was hopping on one foot and holding the other off the ground. When his protected foot chanced to touch down, I could hear him grunt with pain.

"Right," I said. "Just help him up onto the table. I'll look after him."

Terry bade me good day and hurried back out and off to the station. I could see even before taking off the young man's boot and sock and rolling up his heather-tweed pant leg that he had a serious sprain in his ankle. It was swollen but not otherwise misshapen and most likely needed no more than some cold compresses, a tight bandage, and keeping off of it for a week. He also had a bandage wrapped around his hand, and some blood had seeped through it. Must have had a nasty fall and done damage to both hand and foot.

"Please, Doctor," he said. "Please. Just wrap it up and give me a bit of morphine and a pair of crutches. I have to be on my way. I have terribly urgent business to attend to."

"Very well," I said. "Keep your head back on the table, and I will do just that."

With a sterilized needle and syringe, I injected a generous shot of morphine into his upper arm. It was more than what was needed to quell the pain, and within a couple of minutes, it had the desired effect of soothing his spirit as well as his body. I brought some ice from out of the chest, wrapped it, and held it against the ankle and was relieved to see the swelling diminish. I took the bandage off his hand and saw that the blood had come from a straight cut. He must have landed on a shard of glass as he fell. It was not so deep as to need sutures, so I just cleaned it up and applied a tight carbolized bandage.

My patient continued to lie on his back, staring up at the ceiling with vacant eyes. After some ten minutes passed, he lifted his head and spoke to me.

"Thank you, doctor. That is much better. I was in terrible pain."

"Much of that," I said, "you brought on by trying to walk after you had injured yourself. You should have just sat down and called for help."

"I could not do that. I had to keep going. I cannot stay here any longer. My situation is urgent."

"I am sure it is, but you will not go far without a pair of crutches, and I will not get them for you for another five minutes. But I will organize a cup of tea and some nourishment. And then you will be able to move faster than ever and make up for whatever time you are delayed here. Meanwhile, young man, tell me what it is that is distressing you."

For a moment, I thought he was going to argue with me, but he nodded, sat up on the edge of the table and stretched his limbs.

"My mother has gone missing. I have to find her. I fear something untoward has happened to her."

"You don't say. Usually, it's mothers who are desperately looking for their sons. They themselves do not wander off. I am sure she will be back shortly. Most likely already waiting for you at home."

"No Doctor. She has been missing now for a week. Something terrible has happened to her."

"Oh dear. Have you contacted the police?"

"I went immediately to the local police in Reading and reported it. They laughed in my face and told me to go home and wait for her."

"Rather rude of them. Not at all what I would expect from the Reading constabulary," I said.

"Now I am on my way to Scotland Yard. As soon as you can help me with a pair of crutches, I will be on my way."

"Good heavens, man. Scotland Yard will only look into something if they have evidence that there is some serious criminal concern. They aren't likely to send their inspectors off on a search for a missing mom."

"But it is criminal. She has been kidnapped. I am sure of it. And her life is in danger." There was obvious anguish in the fellow's voice, and I sought to calm his spirit.

"Oh, come now. You mustn't horrify me. Why would you think such things?"

"Because last night, at her home just outside Reading, two men tried to kill me. They were in her house when I arrived, and one of them came after me with a knife. I held him off, but he took a nick out of my hand. The other one drew a pistol, and I ran away. I went straight for the woods as I used to run harrier in school and escaped them, but in running, I came to a fallen tree. It was high, but I thought I could jump it. I did not clear it and fell and hurt my ankle. That is why the railway man brought me here. But now I have to get to Scotland Yard and see if they will help me. If they will not then, I do not know what to do. She is in terrible danger. I know she is."

For the first time since he had arrived, I took a close look at his face and remarked to myself that he was a singularly unattractive young male. His face was oddly unbalanced with one eye sunken and hooded and the other protruding and slightly askew. His nose was too large for his narrow head and small mouth and, most striking of all, on the left side of his face was a large wine-colored birthmark that extended from his temple all the way to his neck before disappearing under his collar. He was not sickly in any way. I could tell by my grip on his calf muscle that his body was taut and conditioned by strenuous exercise. He effortlessly pushed himself off the table, balanced on his one good foot and reached into his suit pocket, and brought out his card and handed it to me.

It read: Victor Hatherley, Ph.D. Hydraulic Engineer. Department of Engineering. University of Cambridge.

Below it was an address on Victoria Street in Cambridge.

By this time in my life, I had already seen scores of people enter the presence of Sherlock Holmes in his Baker Street rooms and had a rather good sense of those who were in serious straights and those who were no more than a few bricks short of a full load. I knew right off that Mr. Hatherley was in the first lot.

"When you get to Scotland Yard," I said. "I suggest that you ask to see Inspector Lestrade. He is a bit on the brusque side but generally competent. If anyone can help you, he can."

The lad looked at me with his sunken eye directed toward my eyes and the other one toward my right ear. "How is it that you are familiar with Scotland Yard? What if this inspector will not listen to me?"

"I have had a few dealings with them over the years. And if he will not attend to your case, then I have another suggestion."

"Yes?"

"Have you heard of the detective, Mr. Sherlock Holmes?"

"Yes. I have heard of that fellow. I read about him in *The Strand.* You know, all those exaggerated sensational stories that make him seem superhuman."

"He happens to be a friend of mine. If Scotland Yard will not be of help, then come back to me, and I will see if he can take you on."

He gave me a bit of a look and then glanced up at my medical diploma on the wall and nodded. A blush came to the side of his face that was not already colored.

"You're …?"

"I am indeed. The exaggerating sensationalist and happy to assist you, Dr. Hatherley. Now be on your way. One of those cabs over there will take you to The Embankment. And do come back if you need to."

Chapter Two

Mom is Missing

The remainder of the day passed uneventfully. I was visited by a gaggle of nannies with their coughing and running-nosed children, by two young mothers-to-be who had been sent by husbands that clearly did not have sufficient basic intelligence to know that there is nothing healthier on God's good earth than a young woman in the mid-term of her expectancy. There were also two elderly retired railwaymen who were bent over and wobbling but who could not refrain from telling me the most outrageous and hilarious stories of medical emergencies that had taken place in the nation's rail cars. By four o'clock, the waiting room had emptied, and I was walking out my door and on my way home when I heard my name being called. Moving quite rapidly down the pavement, I saw a young man taking first a long stride on a pair of crutches followed by an athletic hop on his one good leg. Within a few seconds, he was standing in front of me.

"No help from Scotland Yard?" I asked, although his presence had already answered my question.

"No. I had to wait for several hours before getting to see Inspector Lestrade. He laughed at me as well and sent me off."

This struck me as out of character for Lestrade. He never laughed at anything, and his reported reaction seemed a bit odd. I thought it quite possible that there was some facet of young Victor

Hatherley's story that I had failed to perceive, and I feared that I would be doing no more than wasting the time of Sherlock Holmes. However, I had told the chap I would help him, and so I hailed a hansom, and we made our way along Marylebone Road and over to 221B Baker Street.

Mrs. Hudson welcomed me like a long-lost prodigal son. I made my way up our seventeen steps, followed by the young engineer, who managed them surprisingly well for a man on a brace of crutches. Sherlock Holmes was sitting in his customary armchair reading what appeared to be a scientific journal of some sort, sipping on a snifter of brandy, and enjoying his beloved pipe. He rose and welcomed me.

"Ah, my dear Watson. How goes the battle? Married life is treating you well, I must say. I have never seen you looking so fulfilled." He gave a pat with the back of his hand to my midriff section that, I must confess, was not suffering. He offered to have Mrs. Hudson bring us an early supper, but I declined, saying that I would return to my home and my wife shortly but came only to introduce a young man in need of the unique special services that were his exclusive province and introduced him to Victor Hatherley.

"Please, then be seated," he said graciously and turned to the young man who had accompanied me.

"Let me begin by asking the obvious," said Holmes. I assumed that he was about to question Victor concerning his foot, but I winced in outrage at the question he posed instead.

"What orphanage did you grow up in? Most likely, one on the East Side. Stepney Causeway, perhaps. Ah yes. You are a Bernardo boy."

The young man looked surprised, as had many men before and after him who had sat in the same chair and been introduced to Sherlock Holmes.

"Yes, sir. I am a Bernardo boy."

"Of course, you are. With a face like yours, no mother would want you, and you were left on the good Dr. Bernardo's doorstep. But then someone did adopt you. Your clothes and bearing, your accent, and your athleticism all say that at some point, somebody took pity on you and took you home and raised you. And now my dear friend Doctor Watson has brought you to see me so you must be in dire straits else he would not have done so. Either your situation is not appropriate for Scotland Yard, or you tried, and they have refused to help. Ah yes, the latter, your good eye says so. I do believe that we have an interesting case being presented to us, Watson. What say you?"

"I say, Holmes, that your utter tactlessness is appalling. If it were not that Dr. Hatherley is in need of your help, I would leave with him this instant and give him my deepest apologies for introducing him to you."

Holmes looked authentically surprised at my rebuke.

"Good heavens. At what are you taking offense? I welcomed the lad, offered food and drink and a comfortable chair. Now I am respecting the time of both of you and not wasting it with meaningless chit-chat."

There was no point arguing. I shrugged and continued. "Dr. Hatherley believes that his mother has been kidnapped and is in danger. Last night he was attacked and chased by men with guns. He escaped, even with his injury, and is now seeking your help, having been turned down by the Reading police and Lestrade."

"Ah, my afternoon has, at last, become interesting. Please, young man, state your case. How do you know that your mother is in peril? Many wives and mothers of all ages have fits of goodness knows what, leave their husbands and children for any number of reasons good and bad, and then they come home again having accepted their lot in life. I have seen it many times. Why should I think yours would be any different? Before answering that, please introduce yourself more fully."

Victor hesitated before speaking and looked intently at Holmes but then responded.

"You are quite right, sir, in your insights. My mother did adopt me when I was eight years old, and yes, it had been assumed by

Bernardo's that I would be there until I turned sixteen since no family wanted a child with my appearance. My mother said she chose me for my brains, not my face, and in the past seventeen years, my mother and I developed an exceptional bond between us. A day does not pass that we are not in contact with each other. She has traveled the world, sometimes taking me with her and, at other times sending telegrams back to me daily. She has never, not once sir, disappeared for over a week without informing me of her whereabouts. She would never do that to me as I would never do it to her. We are just too close to each other."

"And who is this mother of yours?" asked Holmes. "The loving and devoted Mrs. Hatherley?"

"That is not my mother's name," said Victor. "My mom is Gertrude Margaret Ring. I assume that you have heard of her."

I came close to joining the Reading police and Lestrade in breaking out into laughter. Of course, we had heard of her. Everyone had heard of her. She had made sure of that. Gertrude Ring had been in the public eye for over forty years and was one of the most outrageous women in the Empire. Ostensibly a reporter for *The Times* and widely believed to be a reckless adventuress and likely a spy (for which side no one was sure), she had been present at countless notable events and written stories for the press and several books. Although I had never met her personally, she and I were fellow contributors to *The Strand*. She had been present recently when the Brooklyn Bridge had opened and again six days later when a wild crowd heard that the bridge was about to collapse and stampeded, killing a dozen men, women and children. She had urged the Foreign Office to block King Leopold of Belgium's appropriating the entire Congo as his personal fiefdom, and had presciently warned that General Chinese Gordon was undertaking an arrogant mission to the Sudan that would end in disaster. Just this past year, she rode the Canadian Pacific Railway across the entire length of Canada, stopping only to watch as the last spike, completing the sea-to-sea rail line, was driven in the remote Rocky Mountain village of Craigellachie. It was reported that she had to show Lord Strathcona how to hold a sledgehammer. She was friends with Susan B. Anthony and with both mother and daughter Pankhurst. Her name had been linked romantically with royalty throughout Europe, with captains of industry on both sides of the Atlantic, and with the most dashing actors in the West End. There were many stories of her daring escapes on horseback, camelback, foot, canoe, and rowing shell from men who were shooting at her. That she would have run off one more time while armed men were in pursuit was no surprise whatsoever, and I was about to say so in a most blustering manner when I caught a sharp look from Holmes that bid me hold my tongue.

"I have heard of your mother. She is a remarkable woman, and I do recall some stories in the press years ago concerning her adopting an orphan child. It caused a bit of a stir."

"It did," said Victor. "Many upright people were offended that a single woman with such a way of living should be allowed to raise a child. They claimed that it was one more of her publicity stunts. She would have been denied the right to adopt except that she went to Dr. Bernardo and asked him for the most unwanted child in his homes, and he gave her me. That silenced her critics since they could not claim that she had taken away an opportunity for me to have been placed in a normal and proper family. She has admitted to me that I was her project that year. She had turned fifty years old and proven over and over that a woman could do anything a man could do. But of course, there was one thing that a woman could do that a man could not, and that was to give birth and create a new life. She had missed her opportunity but decided that she would do the next best thing and raise a child on her own. I was needed as an exhibit."

"And somewhere along the way, that changed, did it not?" queried Holmes.

"For the first three months she was at my side twenty-four hours of the day, but she soon tired of that. So I was provided with the most progressive tutors and governesses and subjected to every passing fad and whim in child-rearing, education, nutrition, and physical training. She could not stand to be confined to an ordinary life of a mother in England, so she dragged me along with her all over the world. I tolerated it, happy to be out of the orphanage and grateful for the opportunity that God had given me even if it were with a very strange woman who now claimed to be my mother."

"And then?" asked Holmes.

"What can I say? We began to care for each other and eventually became fanatically loyal to each other. She came to love me as only a mother can love and adore her only son, and I would have walked over hot coals for her; I would die to protect her. We are still that way. We know each other's thoughts before we can express them. We finish each other's sentences. We immediately are attracted to each other's true friends and ready to pick up cudgels with each other's critics. We are never inconsiderate of each other, and neither of us would think of letting a week go by without the other knowing our whereabouts."

"Your mother," said Holmes, "has not been in the press much in the recent past. Why is that?"

"In part because she is now sixty-five years old and has slowed done somewhat, but mostly because she has been helping me in my work at Cambridge."

Again Sherlock Holmes paused before speaking. "I believe I also recall some mention of Gertrude Ring's son being admitted to Cambridge at a very young age. Did not the Press compare you to Francis Bacon?"

"They did, and it was nonsense. I never attended a public school, but I wrote the entrance examinations and was admitted when I was sixteen. School was not difficult for me, and I completed the third part of my Tripos when I was twenty-one. I admit I did well and was the Senior Wrangler for that year. The university has kept me on, and I now work in the new Department of Engineering."

"Excellent," said Holmes. "Would that be under the direction of Professors Stewart, Ewing and Parsons and the rest of the wizards?"

"Charles Parsons is the director of the project, but in my work, I am reporting to his assistant, Professor Stark."

"And you say your mother was helping you? Most mothers of college lads are happy to have them out of the home and would never dream of following them to school. What in heaven's name are you doing up there that could be of any interest to your mother? Steam turbines are not the usual province of women in their seventh decade of life."

"You are aware then of the work done by Dr. Parsons?"

"I have some knowledge of it. Please explain your area of research to me, and do your best to be concise and precise."

Most young scientists and engineers are only too eager to tell anyone who will listen about their particular field of endeavor, even to those who are only feigning interest. To be so asked by England's most famous detective should have occasioned a deluge of passionate babbling. Yet that did not happen. Victor Hatherley said nothing and looked altogether ill at ease.

"You have put me into a difficult situation, sir. I can only say that I am certain that she has been kidnapped, and it is directly connected to our work at Cambridge, but the project that I am working on with my mother and a very select group of colleagues has been commissioned by the Admiralty and is classed as secret. I could be tried for treason if I were to divulge it to you."

I could swear that saw a flash of a spontaneous smile appear for a second on the face of Sherlock Holmes. Even I could now discern that this case had acquired an appeal far beyond the tracking of an aged and wandering parent. Holmes recovered his stone face and continued.

"Indeed. Well then, we shall not act in any way that might offend Her Majesty's government. It is enough to deduce that your secret assignment has to do with the application of steam turbines to our warships in such a manner as to give the Empire some sort of naval advantage. As my reasoning is no more than the application of common sense, I do not believe that a nod from you would constitute treason."

The young engineer looked uneasily at Holmes and then nodded.

"And might I further reason," Holmes continued, "that your mother, brilliant woman as she is, was not assisting with the design and the science but with the necessary harassing of the mandarins in Whitehall, the politicians in Westminster, and the Lords of the Admiralty. Someone has to make sure that the necessary monies and approvals keep flowing else all research grinds to a halt."

"Yes, sir. That is indeed her role."

"Ah ha. An important secret project indeed. But why would anyone want to kidnap your mom? She is an exceptional person, but if she has no expertise related to the science and engineering involved, what benefit is she to anyone?"

"Sir, I do not know. I have been asking myself that question all day. There is no explanation for it. Quite frankly, sir, anyone foolish enough to take my mom captive would be inviting no end of pain and suffering into his life. She would see to that."

Holmes and I both chuckled and Holmes continued.

"There is an explanation. It is perfectly obvious and the only one that makes any sense at all."

"Sir?"

"Whoever has taken your mother has no interest in her. They are after you."

"Me?"

"You are the one with the complete understanding of the engineering behind your secret project. Your devoted attachment to your mother must have been known to all with whom you have ever been associated. It was inevitable that when you did not hear from her that you would come looking for her. It was easy to find her home near Reading and remove her from it and then just wait for you to show up."

"If that was their plan, then I fell into the trap."

"Yes, and they were not trying to kill you, else they would have succeeded. One of them came at you with a knife. If he had any training at all - and I assume that you have had none - he could have plunged it into you. The second man had a gun and must have been close enough to put a bullet into your head but did not do so. What they had not banked on was your skill and speed as a harrier runner. Running at speed through a forest is something no sensible man will attempt, let alone excel at."

Here Holmes paused. "Permit me to digress for a moment. How did you happen to become so proficient at that sport? Only a few young men go out for it. The others all try out for the rowing, cricket, rugby, or football teams. What drove you to such a demanding pastime?"

Victor shrugged. "Do you really need to ask?"

Holmes again laughed. "Of course not. Your mother."

"Yes. Because of my appearance and everyone knowing that I was a Bernardo boy, my mother realized that I would be ostracized and blocked from any of the popular team sports. She said that there were far too many insufferable snobbish twits on those teams and that I had to take up a sport that relied on my skills and wits alone. So I went out for harrier. To it, I now owe my freedom, if what you say is correct, and I have to admit that it makes sense."

"Young man, it is a truth of both advanced experimental science as well as basic detective work that when all other possibilities have been disproven, the only one remaining, however improbable, must be the truth."

"I will remember that, sir. But what now? I escaped. Someone still has my mother. I am still in dread that she will be killed. I would go now and give myself up and take her place if I thought that doing so would save her."

"Oh my goodness, young man. No. That will not do. Really, my boy, if you were to throw in the towel that quickly, how would your mother react? I dare say she would box your ears, and kick your backside across the Thames and back again. Am I correct?"

"Yes, sir. She was always impatient with me when I failed to use my brain. But what then do I do?"

"Nothing. You wait. You wait for whoever has taken your mother to act. They failed to capture you on their first attempt. They will act again very soon."

"Mr. Holmes. I cannot just sit and do nothing. I will go mad with worry. Please, sir, you have to come up with some sort of plan to find her and rescue her. I put my case into your hands and shall do exactly what you advise, but you must tell me what happens next?"

"In the very near future – within this week most likely – you will receive some sort of communication from whoever is holding your mother. They will say that you must come and meet with them or they will do terrible things to her if you do not comply and even worse if you go to Scotland Yard. They will give you some sort of means for communicating back to them, and you will do so in an anguished tone stating that you believe that your mother is already dead and demand that they prove that she is alive and well. We may have to repeat this dance several times over the next week or two. It will give us ample opportunity to allow them to furnish us with all of the clues and time we need to bring about their undoing and your mom safely home. And now, young man, I suggest that you get back on your crutches and hobble your way back to Cambridge. You have important work to do there."

"Sir. You can't just send me back there. I will go mad with not knowing what is happening. I will be useless in the lab. What you are saying is impossible."

"Oh dear, my boy. I am not sending you back there alone. Dr. Watson and I are coming along with you."

Chapter Three

We Go to Cambridge

herlock Holmes has never passed uneventfully. I was visited by a gaggle of nannies with their coughing and running-nosed children, by two young mothers-to-be who had been sent by husbands that clearly did not have sufficient basic intelligence to know that there is nothing healthier on God's good earth than a young woman in the mid-term of her expectancy. There were also two elderly retired railwaymen who were bent over and wobbling but who could not refrain from telling me the most outrageous and hilarious stories of medical emergencies that had taken place in the nation's rail cars. By four o'clock, the waiting room had emptied, and I was walking out my door and on my way home when I heard my name being called. Moving quite rapidly down the pavement, I saw a young man taking first a long stride on a pair of crutches followed by an athletic hop on his one good leg. Within a few seconds, he was standing in front of me.

"No help from Scotland Yard?" I asked, although his presence had already answered my question.

"No. I had to wait for several hours before getting to see Inspector Lestrade. He laughed at me as well and sent me off."

This struck me as out of character for Lestrade. He never laughed at anything, and his reported reaction seemed a bit odd. I thought it quite possible that there was some facet of young Victor

Hatherley's story that I had failed to perceive, and I feared that I would be doing no more than wasting the time of Sherlock Holmes. However, I had told the chap I would help him, and so I hailed a hansom, and we made our way along Marylebone Road and over to 221B Baker Street.

Mrs. Hudson welcomed me like a long-lost prodigal son. I made my way up our seventeen steps, followed by the young engineer, who managed them surprisingly well for a man on a brace of crutches. Sherlock Holmes was sitting in his customary armchair reading what appeared to be a scientific journal of some sort, sipping on a snifter of brandy, and enjoying his beloved pipe. He rose and welcomed me.

"Ah, my dear Watson. How goes the battle? Married life is treating you well, I must say. I have never seen you looking so fulfilled." He gave a pat with the back of his hand to my midriff section that, I must confess, was not suffering. He offered to have Mrs. Hudson bring us an early supper, but I declined, saying that I would return to my home and my wife shortly but came only to introduce a young man in need of the unique special services that were his exclusive province and introduced him to Victor Hatherley.

"Please, then be seated," he said graciously and turned to the young man who had accompanied me.

"Let me begin by asking the obvious," said Holmes. I assumed that he was about to question Victor concerning his foot, but I winced in outrage at the question he posed instead.

"What orphanage did you grow up in? Most likely, one on the East Side. Stepney Causeway, perhaps. Ah yes. You are a Bernardo boy. "

The young man looked surprised, as had many men before and after him who had sat in the same chair and been introduced to Sherlock Holmes.

"Yes, sir. I am a Bernardo boy."

"Of course, you are. With a face like yours, no mother would want you, and you were left on the good Dr. Bernardo's doorstep. But then someone did adopt you. Your clothes and bearing, your accent, and your athleticism all say that at some point, somebody took pity on you and took you home and raised you. And now my dear friend Doctor Watson has brought you to see me so you must be in dire straits else he would not have done so. Either your situation is not appropriate for Scotland Yard, or you tried, and they have refused to help. Ah yes, the latter, your good eye says so. I do believe that we have an interesting case being presented to us, Watson. What say you?"

"I say, Holmes, that your utter tactlessness is appalling. If it were not that Dr. Hatherley is in need of your help, I would leave with him this instant and give him my deepest apologies for introducing him to you."

Holmes looked authentically surprised at my rebuke.

"Good heavens. At what are you taking offense? I welcomed the lad, offered food and drink and a comfortable chair. Now I am respecting the time of both of you and not wasting it with meaningless chit-chat."

There was no point arguing. I shrugged and continued. "Dr. Hatherley believes that his mother has been kidnapped and is in danger. Last night he was attacked and chased by men with guns. He escaped, even with his injury, and is now seeking your help, having been turned down by the Reading police and Lestrade."

"Ah, my afternoon has, at last, become interesting. Please, young man, state your case. How do you know that your mother is in peril? Many wives and mothers of all ages have fits of goodness knows what, leave their husbands and children for any number of reasons good and bad, and then they come home again having accepted their lot in life. I have seen it many times. Why should I think yours would be any different? Before answering that, please introduce yourself more fully."

Victor hesitated before speaking and looked intently at Holmes but then responded.

"You are quite right, sir, in your insights. My mother did adopt me when I was eight years old, and yes, it had been assumed by

Bernardo's that I would be there until I turned sixteen since no family wanted a child with my appearance. My mother said she chose me for my brains, not my face, and in the past seventeen years, my mother and I developed an exceptional bond between us. A day does not pass that we are not in contact with each other. She has traveled the world, sometimes taking me with her and, at other times sending telegrams back to me daily. She has never, not once sir, disappeared for over a week without informing me of her whereabouts. She would never do that to me as I would never do it to her. We are just too close to each other."

"And who is this mother of yours?" asked Holmes. "The loving and devoted Mrs. Hatherley?"

"That is not my mother's name," said Victor. "My mom is Gertrude Margaret Ring. I assume that you have heard of her."

I came close to joining the Reading police and Lestrade in breaking out into laughter. Of course, we had heard of her. Everyone had heard of her. She had made sure of that. Gertrude Ring had been in the public eye for over forty years and was one of the most outrageous women in the Empire. Ostensibly a reporter for *The Times* and widely believed to be a reckless adventuress and likely a spy (for which side no one was sure), she had been present at countless notable events and written stories for the press and several books. Although I had never met her personally, she and I were fellow contributors to *The Strand*. She had been present recently when the Brooklyn Bridge had opened and again six days later when a wild crowd heard that the bridge was about to collapse and stampeded, killing a dozen men, women and children. She had urged the Foreign Office to block King Leopold of Belgium's appropriating the entire Congo as his personal fiefdom, and had presciently warned that General Chinese Gordon was undertaking an arrogant mission to the Sudan that would end in disaster. Just this past year, she rode the Canadian Pacific Railway across the entire length of Canada, stopping only to watch as the last spike, completing the sea-to-sea rail line, was driven in the remote Rocky Mountain village of Craigellachie. It was reported that she had to show Lord Strathcona how to hold a sledgehammer. She was friends with Susan B. Anthony and with both mother and daughter Pankhurst. Her name had been linked romantically with royalty throughout Europe, with captains of industry on both sides of the Atlantic, and with the most dashing actors in the West End. There were many stories of her daring escapes on horseback, camelback, foot, canoe, and rowing shell from men who were shooting at her. That she would have run off one more time while armed men were in pursuit was no surprise whatsoever, and I was about to say so in a most blustering manner when I caught a sharp look from Holmes that bid me hold my tongue.

"I have heard of your mother. She is a remarkable woman, and I do recall some stories in the press years ago concerning her adopting an orphan child. It caused a bit of a stir."

"It did," said Victor. "Many upright people were offended that a single woman with such a way of living should be allowed to raise a child. They claimed that it was one more of her publicity stunts. She would have been denied the right to adopt except that she went to Dr. Bernardo and asked him for the most unwanted child in his homes, and he gave her me. That silenced her critics since they could not claim that she had taken away an opportunity for me to have been placed in a normal and proper family. She has admitted to me that I was her project that year. She had turned fifty years old and proven over and over that a woman could do anything a man could do. But of course, there was one thing that a woman could do that a man could not, and that was to give birth and create a new life. She had missed her opportunity but decided that she would do the next best thing and raise a child on her own. I was needed as an exhibit."

"And somewhere along the way, that changed, did it not?" queried Holmes.

"For the first three months she was at my side twenty-four hours of the day, but she soon tired of that. So I was provided with the most progressive tutors and governesses and subjected to every passing fad and whim in child-rearing, education, nutrition, and physical training. She could not stand to be confined to an ordinary life of a mother in England, so she dragged me along with her all over the world. I tolerated it, happy to be out of the orphanage and grateful for the opportunity that God had given me even if it were with a very strange woman who now claimed to be my mother."

"And then?" asked Holmes.

"What can I say? We began to care for each other and eventually became fanatically loyal to each other. She came to love me as only a mother can love and adore her only son, and I would have walked over hot coals for her; I would die to protect her. We are still that way. We know each other's thoughts before we can express them. We finish each other's sentences. We immediately are attracted to each other's true friends and ready to pick up cudgels with each other's critics. We are never inconsiderate of each other, and neither of us would think of letting a week go by without the other knowing our whereabouts."

"Your mother," said Holmes, "has not been in the press much in the recent past. Why is that?"

"In part because she is now sixty-five years old and has slowed done somewhat, but mostly because she has been helping me in my work at Cambridge."

Again Sherlock Holmes paused before speaking. "I believe I also recall some mention of Gertrude Ring's son being admitted to Cambridge at a very young age. Did not the Press compare you to Francis Bacon?"

"They did, and it was nonsense. I never attended a public school, but I wrote the entrance examinations and was admitted when I was sixteen. School was not difficult for me, and I completed the third part of my Tripos when I was twenty-one. I admit I did well and was the Senior Wrangler for that year. The university has kept me on, and I now work in the new Department of Engineering."

"Excellent," said Holmes. "Would that be under the direction of Professors Stewart, Ewing and Parsons and the rest of the wizards?"

"Charles Parsons is the director of the project, but in my work, I am reporting to his assistant, Professor Stark."

"And you say your mother was helping you? Most mothers of college lads are happy to have them out of the home and would never dream of following them to school. What in heaven's name are you doing up there that could be of any interest to your mother? Steam turbines are not the usual province of women in their seventh decade of life."

"You are aware then of the work done by Dr. Parsons?"

"I have some knowledge of it. Please explain your area of research to me, and do your best to be concise and precise."

Most young scientists and engineers are only too eager to tell anyone who will listen about their particular field of endeavor, even to those who are only feigning interest. To be so asked by England's most famous detective should have occasioned a deluge of passionate babbling. Yet that did not happen. Victor Hatherley said nothing and looked altogether ill at ease.

"You have put me into a difficult situation, sir. I can only say that I am certain that she has been kidnapped, and it is directly connected to our work at Cambridge, but the project that I am working on with my mother and a very select group of colleagues has been commissioned by the Admiralty and is classed as secret. I could be tried for treason if I were to divulge it to you."

I could swear that saw a flash of a spontaneous smile appear for a second on the face of Sherlock Holmes. Even I could now discern that this case had acquired an appeal far beyond the tracking of an aged and wandering parent. Holmes recovered his stone face and continued.

"Indeed. Well then, we shall not act in any way that might offend Her Majesty's government. It is enough to deduce that your secret assignment has to do with the application of steam turbines to our warships in such a manner as to give the Empire some sort of naval advantage. As my reasoning is no more than the application of common sense, I do not believe that a nod from you would constitute treason."

The young engineer looked uneasily at Holmes and then nodded.

"And might I further reason," Holmes continued, "that your mother, brilliant woman as she is, was not assisting with the design and the science but with the necessary harassing of the mandarins in Whitehall, the politicians in Westminster, and the Lords of the Admiralty. Someone has to make sure that the necessary monies and approvals keep flowing else all research grinds to a halt."

"Yes, sir. That is indeed her role."

"Ah ha. An important secret project indeed. But why would anyone want to kidnap your mom? She is an exceptional person, but if she has no expertise related to the science and engineering involved, what benefit is she to anyone?"

"Sir, I do not know. I have been asking myself that question all day. There is no explanation for it. Quite frankly, sir, anyone foolish enough to take my mom captive would be inviting no end of pain and suffering into his life. She would see to that."

Holmes and I both chuckled and Holmes continued.

"There is an explanation. It is perfectly obvious and the only one that makes any sense at all."

"Sir?"

"Whoever has taken your mother has no interest in her. They are after you."

"Me?"

"You are the one with the complete understanding of the engineering behind your secret project. Your devoted attachment to your mother must have been known to all with whom you have ever been associated. It was inevitable that when you did not hear from her that you would come looking for her. It was easy to find her home near Reading and remove her from it and then just wait for you to show up."

"If that was their plan, then I fell into the trap."

"Yes, and they were not trying to kill you, else they would have succeeded. One of them came at you with a knife. If he had any training at all - and I assume that you have had none - he could have plunged it into you. The second man had a gun and must have been close enough to put a bullet into your head but did not do so. What they had not banked on was your skill and speed as a harrier runner. Running at speed through a forest is something no sensible man will attempt, let alone excel at."

Here Holmes paused. "Permit me to digress for a moment. How did you happen to become so proficient at that sport? Only a few young men go out for it. The others all try out for the rowing, cricket, rugby, or football teams. What drove you to such a demanding pastime?"

Victor shrugged. "Do you really need to ask?"

Holmes again laughed. "Of course not. Your mother."

"Yes. Because of my appearance and everyone knowing that I was a Bernardo boy, my mother realized that I would be ostracized and blocked from any of the popular team sports. She said that there were far too many insufferable snobbish twits on those teams and that I had to take up a sport that relied on my skills and wits alone. So I went out for harrier. To it, I now owe my freedom, if what you say is correct, and I have to admit that it makes sense."

"Young man, it is a truth of both advanced experimental science as well as basic detective work that when all other possibilities have been disproven, the only one remaining, however improbable, must be the truth."

"I will remember that, sir. But what now? I escaped. Someone still has my mother. I am still in dread that she will be killed. I would go now and give myself up and take her place if I thought that doing so would save her."

"Oh my goodness, young man. No. That will not do. Really, my boy, if you were to throw in the towel that quickly, how would your mother react? I dare say she would box your ears, and kick your backside across the Thames and back again. Am I correct?"

"Yes, sir. She was always impatient with me when I failed to use my brain. But what then do I do?"

"Nothing. You wait. You wait for whoever has taken your mother to act. They failed to capture you on their first attempt. They will act again very soon."

"Mr. Holmes. I cannot just sit and do nothing. I will go mad with worry. Please, sir, you have to come up with some sort of plan to find her and rescue her. I put my case into your hands and shall do exactly what you advise, but you must tell me what happens next?"

"In the very near future – within this week most likely – you will receive some sort of communication from whoever is holding your mother. They will say that you must come and meet with them or they will do terrible things to her if you do not comply and even worse if you go to Scotland Yard. They will give you some sort of means for communicating back to them, and you will do so in an anguished tone stating that you believe that your mother is already dead and demand that they prove that she is alive and well. We may have to repeat this dance several times over the next week or two. It will give us ample opportunity to allow them to furnish us with all of the clues and time we need to bring about their undoing and your mom safely home. And now, young man, I suggest that you get back on your crutches and hobble your way back to Cambridge. You have important work to do there."

"Sir. You can't just send me back there. I will go mad with not knowing what is happening. I will be useless in the lab. What you are saying is impossible."

"Oh dear, my boy. I am not sending you back there alone. Dr. Watson and I are coming along with you."

Chapter Four

The Usual Suspects

By the time we reached the second floor on the north end of the old building, the chemical scents had given way to that distinctive smell that I had recently come to associate with the transmission of electricity if one increases the amperage to the point that sparks begin to fly. The office we were led to was situated solidly in the midst of this assault upon the olfactory senses. The nameplate on the door read Colonel Doctor Lysander Stark. The porter knocked and on hearing "*Ja*" opened the door. The office was on the small side and rather long and narrow. On the left-hand wall were bookcases filled with volumes and files from floor to ceiling and arranged so that every one of the several thousand items was aligned at the same angle and the same distance from the edge of the shelf. The other wall held an extensive display of framed certificates, citations, mounted pages from newspapers, and photographs. The earliest items bore the name of Ludwig Zimmerman, but all of the pictures featured the same man, who was also the same chap that was sitting facing us at a desk at the far end of the office. He was not smiling.

He rose as we entered, and I thought that I had never seen a man quite so thin. A bit more good Hertfordshire beef would have done him no harm. He was not, however, unhealthy, and his erect carriage gave evidence of military training at some time in his past.

He motioned us to two chairs in front of his desk but did not come around to greet us.

"*Herr* Sherlock Holmes and Doctor Watson. *Biten,* be seated. I am frightfully busy *heute Morgen*, but a few minutes of my time I have agreed to make. So kindly begin your .. your... *Untersuchung.*" He spoke with a refined German accent and then immediately sat down again and stared at Holmes.

Holmes smiled warmly at the cool professor and spoke. "We do apologize, Colonel Stark, for interrupting your work, but please bear with us, sir. You must understand that it is only because Her Majesty's government views your work as so important that they are bothering to review your procedures for maintaining secrecy. I assure you that the efforts of your colleagues, even the esteemed Professors Stewart and Ewing, have not merited such attention as they are not considered to be of sufficient strategic value to the British Empire. Were it not for the unique and critical nature of the research you are leading, I can tell you, quite frankly, I would not be here."

Professor Stark smiled, and I could see his body relax and incline itself ever so slightly toward Holmes. "We are pleased that in London someone there finally is understanding how significant is the research that here is undertaken. Although I can assure you that guarding confidentiality is not a problem, nevertheless, by your concern, we are encouraged. I assume your visit is caused by the flight of our dear old crazy lady, Miss Ring. She is very useful to us, but highly, we would say, *exzenter.* "Eccentric" is your English word, I believe. She is no doubt over the Matterhorn in a balloon lofting as we speak, and we expect her in a few days to return. Are there other issues, sir? *Biten,* your questions, *Herr* Holmes."

Holmes, using his most respectful manner, proceeded to pose a question concerning the members of the team who had been assigned to the secret project and to ask for reassurance concerning their trustworthiness. The professor responded.

"Let me begin with my capable assistant, Professor Elise Carpenter. She is a brilliant mathematician and engineer. It is a pity she is a woman working in a man's field of endeavor. She has been at

Cambridge since as a student fifteen years ago, she was first admitted. Here at the University is her entire life. Never does she travel anywhere. Of her integrity, there can be no question. As to our clerk and bookkeeper, Mr. Malcolm Ferguson, with respect to engineering and any aspect of any science, he is an imbecile. However, appointed by the Parsons Company, he was and is unquestionably loyal to them to the point of obsessive concern for the reading of every note we make and accounting for every last farthing I spend on the project. Out of necessity, I tolerate his presence.

"I have three younger people also to this project assigned. One has already passed his doctoral examinations, and the others are on their way. Mr. Jeremiah Hayling-Kynynmound is a clever enough *junge* but in his rowboat far more interested than the laboratory. However, he is a useful idiot and capable of doing what he is told in the carrying out the experiments. Then there is our orphan boy, Dr. Victor Hatherley. For someone from such a mongrel lineage, he is quite surprisingly brilliant. He would not dare betray anything related to this project else his mother would flail him within an inch of his life, but, of course, with those of mixed race you can never be entirely sure. What runs in their blood, you have no idea. And then finally, we have Miss Philippa Fawcett. Her mother is a raving suffragette, and the daughter holds similar radical views, but she is sensible enough not in my laboratory to give them voice. Frankly, it is a shame that she also is a woman. Otherwise, she could look forward to being offered a paid position in the University. She is exceptionally bright. What else do you wish to know?"

"I did not hear anything about Miss Ring," said Holmes.

"Our mad woman? She has no need for money and is involved in this project only because of her devotion to her son and his to her. She is useful in our dealings with the *functionars* in Whitehall and the Admiralty. For any insight into her psyche, I suggest that you consult Dr. Freud in Vienna. You have heard of him, I assume, *Herr* Holmes?"

"Indeed, I have, sir. Fortunately, I am only responsible for assessing the risk to official secrecy and not psychological similarities to tragic figures from ancient Greece. So if I may, you have addressed the matter of the competence of your staff, now perhaps you could explain what criteria you used to ascertain whether or not they are people of integrity."

The professor shrugged his boney shoulders. "We know them, and we know their people. Every one of them, except Miss Philippa, here in Cambridge has spent the past ten years or more. We would have known by now whether or not they could be trusted. The only other exception is the clerk, and he, I must believe, to Charles Parsons is well-known or else he would not have been selected."

"Ah, yes. Of course," said Holmes. "That does make sense. Quite logical. But it looks as though you have missed one member. The most important one. The leader of the enterprise."

For a moment, Professor Stark looked at Holmes quizzically, and then his visage changed into outright anger and he shouted, "Are you suggesting that I myself could be suspected? How dare you question my integrity!"

"Oh come, come, professor. That is not it at all. But you must understand that I was sent by Whitehall to report on everybody, and if I failed to include the name of the most important person then, well sir, they would just send me back to do it all over again. You must understand that, sir. So please, no offense. I am reporting to … what do you call them …*functionars* and *regierungsbeamters*?"

The professor's face softened into a thin smile. "Ah, I see that England's famous detective has learned a little German. And yes, I do understand your situation. So very well, *Herr* Holmes, please tell your blokes, I believe that is what you call them, that Professor Lysander Stark is a treacherous spy for the Kaiser and any day now to Berlin with a two-ton steam turbine on his back he may run off." He laughed at his own joke. Holmes smiled in return.

"And you may also remind them that I have in the success of this project an *entgeltliche*, what you in this country call a pecuniary interest. I already own many shares in the new company of Mr. Parsons and an agreement with many more based on the completion and future commercial value of our research I will be rewarded. Is

31

that sufficient information to take to your government to convince them that I am a spy?"

"More than sufficient, and I thank you for your wit. I shall file a report accordingly. Now, as you are the *fuhrer* of this project, may I ask you to select the first of your staff for us to speak with?"

Stark nodded and reached over and pulled on a bell cord. Within seconds, a small, bespectacled woman came scurrying into his office. "Yes, Professor. You called, Professor?"

"Miss Fitzwilliams, go and ask Doctor Carpenter if she could join us."

"Yes Professor," the woman replied and then scurried off again. Less than a minute later, another woman entered the office. I would have placed her age at around thirty-five. Unlike the secretary, this lady was tall, at least as tall as I am and maybe an inch more. Her blonde hair was pulled onto the back of her head, accentuating her beautiful face, flawless pale complexion, and bright blue eyes. I have nowhere near the ability of Sherlock Holmes to read the expression on people's faces, but even I could detect a look of concern and worry on her lovely countenance.

The professor rose from his chair and spoke to us. "Herr Holmes and Doctor Watson, allow me to introduce Doctor Carpenter, one of the most knowledgeable engineers in all of England. We have taken her away from the laboratory where she spends her entire days, and evenings and weekends, and we apologize for doing so, Doctor Carpenter."

The woman engineer did not immediately look at Holmes and me. She kept looking at Stark. I thought I saw a tiny shaking of his head as he looked back directly at her, followed by a flicker of a smile and a nod. It all happened quickly, and she then turned to us with a friendly smile and, with a trace of a Cornwall accent, held out her hand.

"I have heard of you two gentlemen from my students. You have some fans here in Cambridge, even if I cannot claim to be amongst them. Neither can I claim to have been interrogated by a detective before. I do enjoy new adventures and discoveries, however, so please come and join me in the laboratory, and we can have a chat."

"No, no," interjected Stark. "Mr. Holmes has been cleared to speak with us but not to view the laboratory. Why do you not just take him down to the examination hall? It is not being used today and should be quite private."

"Of course, Doctor Stark," the woman replied. "Good suggestion. Thank you, doctor."

She then turned to us and said, "Gentlemen, please follow me." She led us back down a stairwell and into a large cavernous hall at the north end of the building. The entire room was filled with several hundred small individual desks and chairs. Professor Carpenter quickly pushed three of them into a close circle and motioned to Holmes and me to occupy two of them while she sat in the third.

"Gentlemen, I am Elise Carpenter. I direct the project's laboratory and supervise the research fellows working there. How may I be of assistance to you?"

"Madam Professor," Holmes began, "as your time is precious, I will come directly to the point. Concerns have been expressed regarding the ability of your laboratory to continue to carry out highly confidential research that has been assigned to you by the Admiralty. These concerns are of sufficient depth that they reached the ears of certain officials in Whitehall and, as a result, I have been requested to look into the matter and report back."

"I would not have thought that an amateur detective was qualified to do so. Why did they not appoint someone senior from Scotland Yard?"

Holmes held out his hands, palms upward, and affected a sheepish look on his face. "I cannot possibly defend any logic behind a decision by Her Majesty's government and have, on many occasions, been baffled by the utter lack of it. I can only tell you that I received the request, and as a loyal subject of Her Majesty, have complied. I can only beseech you to do the same, and this whole exercise will then be over soon enough."

She smiled back. "Very well. Soon enough. Carry on for Her Majesty, sir."

"What evidence," he began in a matter-of-fact tone, "have you ever observed that Professor Stark may be working as an agent of the government of Germany?"

I was stunned by the bluntness of the question. So was Professor Carpenter. Her eyes widened, and I expected an outraged response. But then I sensed that she checked herself and affected an expression of *qui sait?*

"I am a scientist, and I can only speak to what I have observed and know to be true. I have known Doctor Stark for many years and have never seen any such evidence. However, I have only observed him here at the University. He arrives every day at ten minutes before nine in the morning and leaves at twenty-five minutes past six in the late afternoon. Those are the times I have observed him and can speak to. I have no knowledge of what he does in the evenings or on the weekends, and, again as a scientist, I have learned not to speculate on those things about which I know nothing."

"Ah, yes," agreed Holmes. "Wisely spoken. And how long has it been that you have known Doctor Stark?"

She paused for a moment and stared up at the high windows in the hall while slowly shaking her head. "I suppose if I were to review my diaries and notes, I could give you an exact date, but I cannot recall it at the moment. It has been at least a decade. It was almost immediately after he joined the faculty at Cambridge, and I believe that was over ten years ago. So yes, ten years, maybe slightly more, I would have to say."

"And the two of you have collaborated on quite a few successful studies, have you not?"

"Oh yes, I suppose you could say that. Of course, both of us work with other colleagues as well. Cambridge University has a large number of excellent scholars, and I have been honored to have worked with many of them, as has Colonel Stark."

Holmes nodded his assent. "It is indeed one of the great centers of research and researchers in the world. Please explain something to me. In preparation for this visit, I reviewed the journals of hydraulic and mechanical engineering for the past few years. I observed over two score of papers published under the name of Professor Stark, and in which your role as the senior researcher was credited. I do not recall seeing your name on any other papers as having worked collaboratively with any other scientists. Who else have you worked with?"

For a short but perceptible instant, she did not respond, and then, with quiet assurance answered. "Mr. Holmes, I perceive that you have never lived in the groves of academe. Any research carried out in any laboratory always reports the name of the director of the laboratory as the titular lead author of the published paper. It is how our pecking order works. As Colonel Stark is the director of this institute and as I work here, every paper to which my name is attached is also one to which his name is. That is the way things take place here. You might say that rank has its privileges."

"Ah, yes, and here I thought that these hallowed halls were a world away from the rank and file of Her Majesty's soldiers. Thank you for enlightening me."

Holmes went on to quiz her about the graduate students and research fellow, and she responded, asserting that she had supervised the work of all three of them for several years and considered them diligent and upright although she repeated Professor Stark's assessment of Jeremiah Hayling-Kynynmound.

"Jerry's family, "she said, "is listed in Debrett's as a lower rank family in County Durham. He was born with an excellent brain but a character that lacks seriousness. If he put half the thought and energy into his studies as he does his sports, he would be a great scientist. Instead, he appears to be destined to be a middling one. But it is best for you to form your own opinions of our assistants, Mr. Holmes.

Shall I have Mr. Hayling-Kynynmound come and speak with you next? I am assuming that you have no further questions of me."

"Yes, that would be very helpful," replied Holmes. "Please ask him if he could join us briefly."

Once the lady had departed from the hall, I turned to Holmes. "A bit on the snooty side, I dare say. Mind you, I do not have any sense of their being spies, or kidnappers, or holding back any secrets. Do you, Holmes?"

Sherlock Holmes gave me the same look he had countless times in the past. "Good heavens, Watson. There are times that I despair of your ever being able to see anything past the end of your nose. They are hiding an enormous secret which is as obvious as Nelson in Trafalgar Square, if only you would stop and observe and think."

I was quite taken aback by his tone and was about to demand that he explain this so-called secret, but at that moment a young man entered the room. The first thing to strike me was the way he was dressed. All of the other gentlemen at Cambridge, whether students or faculty, were properly attired with a starched white shirt, clean collar and tie, a respectable jacket and the standard academic gown. This chap entered clad in white flannel trousers, a cricket sweater and shoes that would be appropriate on a sailboat but hardly in a laboratory. He was quite strikingly handsome, with a full head of wavy brown hair and perfectly balanced eyes and strong cheekbones. He flashed a broad smile, and I could see that not a single tooth was out of alignment.

"Crikey," he exclaimed. "Auntie Ellie said it was His Such-and-Suchness the very Sherlock Holmes come to see us. I thought she was either balmy or I was blotto. But blimey, here you are. Don't tell me someone has done in the chaplain, and they've hired you to write a good story about it. Good for the college's reputation in the House of Lords. I had hoped to be famous as an oarsman and here I am about to be known by millions for a bit part in *The Strand*."

He smiled and came forward and shook both of our hands.

"Name's Jeremiah Hayling-Kynynmound. But my friends just call me Jerry and I won't tell you what the rest of this town calls me. So that will just have to do."

"A pleasure to meet you, Master Jerry," said Holmes. "And I have been informed that before long we will be calling you Doctor Jerry. Is that correct?"

"Indeed, it is, sir. All I have to do is write another hundred thousand words, and I'll be finished." He flashed his perfect smile again as he spoke.

"And might I ask," said Holmes, feigning interest, "the topic of your unique and original contribution to the ever-evolving body of scientific knowledge?"

"Nothing fancy, sir. I am just recording and writing up the contributions I have made to this project. It's quite the big thing, and I have done my part, if I do say so myself. Most of it I've already written. I was joshing about the words left to go. Needs a bit of the polishing still, but by this time next year, it should be over and done and published for the world to see."

"I am afraid that you have confused me," said Holmes. "I was told that the specific contents of this project were shrouded in secrecy as they were of top-drawer concern to the Admiralty. How is it that you are going to tell the world all about it?"

"Secret?" the young fellow exclaimed. "My Aunt Fanny. There's not a bloke in this whole building, the jolly porter included, that does not know what we're doing up here. And just so that you can put it in your story, Doctor Watson, I'll tell you. We're trying to re-jig Parson's steam turbine so that it can give direct drive to our battleships. And once we have that one cracked, we're going to attach it to an electrical generator and then use the electricity to drive the props on the boat. So there you have it. Secret's out. Come and arrest me for treason, will they? No fee charged to you, Sherlock Holmes. Mind, I expect to have at least an honorable mention when this all comes out in *The Strand*. I would have even more women wanting to marry me if they thought I helped solve a crime than if I merely won a world medal in single sculls."

For the next fifteen minutes or so, Holmes asked the young chap some rather innocuous questions about the work he had been doing and about rowing and about the disappearance of one of the team members, Miss Gertrude Ring.

"Ah, our dear Miss Ring," said Jerry. "I am awfully fond of the old girl. Quite the lively one she is. But my goodness, she has had more adventures, if that is what you want to call them, than your average clergyman's daughter in the East End. I know that Vic-the-Plum is all dreadful worried about his mom but the rest of us ... well ... we told Vic that he could just look under the nearest member of the Czar's family, and he would likely find his mommy." He laughed at his cruel and tasteless joke.

Holmes waited until the laugh had faded and then looked the young man in the eye and said, "I have a duty to tell you that there have been some rather nasty rumors told about you. Some people claim that you not only employed crammers to help you get through your examinations but that you may have hired one of the students who is attending on scholarship to write your assignments. I believe I should hear your side of that story in order to give a fair and complete report."

Jeremiah Hayling-Kynynmound rolled his eyes and put a most pained expression on his face. "Really, sir. That imbecilic talk has become such a bore. It arose out of nothing more and nothing less than envy and jealousy. That is all it was."

"Could you kindly explain that?" asked Holmes.

"What is there to explain? At the end of my third year, our entire class had an important assignment due, and while the rest of them were cooped up like hermits scribbling away, I went to Stockholm for a splendid regatta, in which I performed rather well. I returned and, within seventy-two hours, wrote the paper, submitted it just before the deadline, and received an excellent grade. No one believed that I could have done it without help, but that is because they do not understand the discipline of both mind and body that comes with dedicating yourself to being the best in the world at your sport. I merely transferred that discipline over to my academic work and

38

succeeded." He raised his right hand and snapped his fingers once as he spoke.

"That must have been an exceptionally strenuous undertaking," observed Holmes.

"Mr. Sherlock Holmes, it was nothing more than what I have read that you do when dedicated to one of your cases. I made copious use of tobacco and coffee and focused on nothing but the task at hand. That is what you do, is it not?"

"It is, and may I commend you on your self-discipline. And I see you looking at your watch. Are we keeping you from another engagement?"

"The lunch hour begins in five minutes. I do not take lunch but instead go to the Boat House and spend most of the hour in training. My coach is waiting, and if I do not show up on time, he will make me do another hundred push-ups at speed. So please excuse me now and give my best wishes to the editors of *The Strand*. I look forward to being in their pages."

He rose and smiled and nodded and moved quickly out the door.

I was about to return to my interrogation of Holmes himself, but the mousey Miss Fitzwilliams appeared and announced that lunch would be served at the High Table in Christ's College in fifteen minutes, and the Fellows and Faculty would be waiting for Holmes and me to appear before starting. On hearing this, I reached for my map of the school as I had no idea of which way to go. Holmes, on the other hand, stood and exited the building and began to zig and zag his way through several narrow laneways. I put the map away and followed. A porter was waiting for us and handed us academic gowns, the compulsory uniform behind the walls of ivy.

The lunch was a pleasant affair with several of the gowned gentlemen showing off their obscure knowledge by challenging Holmes on his use of science. One chap assured him that there had been some rather exciting advances in testing for hemoglobin in the past few months, while another informed him that if he had only used Babbage's calculating machine he could have solved the Musgrave ritual much more speedily. Their strutting their stuff was no surprise as it is a universal tendency of those in academe. What was a surprise was that every one of them appeared to have read all of the stories I had written about the adventures of Sherlock Holmes and committed the details to memory. I fully expected that had I entered any one of the many libraries, I might find well-thumbed back copies of *The Strand* secreted in the stacks.

Once dessert had been cleared, the Master of the College called upon Holmes to speak. Holmes did so and, with more erudite, obscure, and arcane references that even I had imagined he could summon, he delivered an altered version of this favorite lecture, *The Science of Deduction*. For a full half-hour after he had finished, he was peppered with questions and then accompanied back to the Cavendish Laboratories by three aging pedagogues who kept up the barrage. I felt myself wondering, "Do these chaps not have jobs to get back to?" The answer was a bit obvious.

On re-entering the examination hall, we saw a young woman sitting at one of the desks that had been moved to accommodate our inquiries. She was not a particularly attractive lady, but had a friendly rounded face, somewhat protruding eyes, and dark hair pulled up onto the top of her high forehead. She had several files and pinned sets of papers on the desk in front of her. I walked over to meet her.

"Miss Philippa Fawcett, I presume? Awfully sorry to have kept you waiting."

"It is quite all right, Doctor Watson, she replied. "Waiting here with no one else around has given me a rare and precious time to read and study. I have tried to make good use of it. And it is an honor to meet you and the famous Mr. Sherlock Holmes. Your visit to our laboratory is quite unexpected."

"It was," replied Holmes, "somewhat unexpected for us as well. However, measures of national secrecy can force other matters aside and take precedence. Your willingness to accommodate us on such short notice is an act for which we are most grateful."

After some exchanges of pleasantries regarding the very demanding mathematical Tripos that Miss Fawcett was studying for, Holmes asked her many of the same questions he had posed to Jerry and Professor Carpenter. She responded frankly and without any sense of guile. Then Holmes queried her with, "How close had you come to Miss Gertrude Ring? Were you, as two women in what has been claimed to be a man's world, allies to each other?"

She did not hesitate to respond. "I idolized her, sir, in the same way that I have my own mother and Professor Carpenter. Such women, with their magnificent accomplishments, have blazed a trail that cannot be denied. Because of their success against all odds, it will only be a matter of time before the vote, and finally, full and equal rights will be accorded to women."

"I cannot," said Holmes, "comment on the progress of legal changes in that regard, as I have no qualifications to do so. I can most assuredly tell you that beyond a shadow of a doubt, women are every bit as skilled at criminal activity as men, although I suspect that is not the type of equality you are referring to."

Miss Fawcett smiled back. "If we are to be considered equal in all matters, sir, we shall just have to accept the bad along with the good. I do not expect, though, that we will see a Miss Jacquelyn the Ripper come along for a few years yet."

We chuckled, and then Holmes quizzed her more concerning Gertrude Ring.

He said, "Professors Stark and Carpenter have dismissed concern for her disappearance as no more than a tempest in a teapot. Given her indomitable and independent spirit, they say, there is no cause for concern. Are you of the same mind, Miss Fawcett?"

"At first, I was, for the reasons you have stated. During the past few days, though, I have had several conversations with Victor, that is Mr. Hatherley. He is a very clever and sensible man and not given to flights of fancy. And yet he is desperately worried about Miss Ring. I assume you are aware that she is his mother?"

"Indeed, we are," said Holmes, "and we will be meeting with him later this afternoon. You appear to know him quite well. Surely you must have sensed that he can be impulsive. He does have a bit of Gypsy blood in him, does he not?"

Miss Fawcett raised her head sharply and gave Holmes a hard look. It was replaced quickly with a faint smile. "I perceive, sir, that you are testing me. And that, of course, is what a detective must do. And I thank you as it is good training for the examinations I will be facing shortly. To answer your question, however, yes, Mr. Hatherley is deeply and emotionally distressed. He is distraught and distracted, but it is in a way that I have never witnessed before. He is adamant that regardless of whatever adventure his mother has scampered off to in the past, she has never let a day let alone a fortnight pass without sending him word of her whereabouts. As a result, I have come to agree with him that there is something terribly wrong, and I fear for her, as well as for Victor."

After a few more questions, Holmes concluded the interview and thanked Miss Fawcett for her time and concern and then turned to me. "Conducting my questions in a sterile hall restricts the observation of so many details that could be seen in someone's home or office. So we shall not call our final member, the accountant fellow, but go and visit him in his office. I am certain that we will find him close to the bursar's desk and not in the secret laboratory."

That was precisely where we found Mr. Malcolm Ferguson. I knocked on the door, and a thin Scottish voice in response brought us into a tiny windowless office. A slight man of about fifty years of age stood behind a desk and bade us good day. "Please, gentlemen, come in. I am sorry that I do not have extra chairs to offer you, so I fear you will have to stand."

The room was only about ten-foot square and remarkably barren. The desk was empty except for two ledger books and a small decorative clock. An inscribed plate on the base of it read, "For twenty-five years of loyal service." There were no photographs, pictures or other items mounted on the wall. The man himself was dressed in a clean but inexpensive black suit, a simple white shirt and a tartan tie; his only stylish adornment being a large pair of gold cufflinks. They were embossed with the initials 'V' and 'M' and to my taste were a bit gaudy, but many a man has had to wear similar objects that have been presented to him by his wife on the occasion of a birthday or wedding anniversary.

"I am Malcolm Ferguson," he said. "But I assume that you already know that. How may I assist you?"

Holmes proceeded into his now well-rehearsed ingratiating introduction thanking the man for his time and stressing how important the project was to Her Majesty's government.

"I am aware of all that, sir," Mr. Ferguson said in a flat voice. "Now, how may I help you?"

Holmes asked him a series of questions respecting the sources of income received and the expenses paid out. He answered by quoting sums to the pence and all without consulting his books or notes.

Holmes asked about Miss Ring and if there had ever been any hints of impropriety with respect to financial affairs in her actions to date concerning this project.

"No, sir."

"Any indication that she was in financial difficulty and needing funds?"

"No, sir."

"Was she worth what she was paid?"

"She wasn't paid, sir."

"She did all this work without receiving a farthing?"

"Yes, sir."

"Is that not rather unusual? I assume that the Parsons Company is not short of funds with which to remunerate its employees and contractors."

"Yes, sir. That is correct. They have more than sufficient."

"Was Miss Ring able to secure additional funds for the project from within Whitehall?"

"Yes, sir."

"And approximately how much was she able to obtain? You do not have to be exact. Just the nearest rounded amount."

"To date, sir, nine thousand six hundred and sixty-nine pounds."

"My that is quite a substantial sum."

"Yes, sir."

"Is that not a very large budget on which to carry out a project at Cambridge?"

"I cannot say, sir. This is the first time I have had anything to do with a project conducted in cooperation with a university."

I kept jotting notes as Holmes asked his questions, but I had concluded soon after we entered this office that this interview was a waste of time. The morose Scotsman was no better than a Babbage's calculating machine. He would spit out the correct number, and that was it. Holmes, who I have seen become most impatient and demanding, carried on serenely until he had exhausted his questions. He thanked the fellow for his time, and we departed.

"Merciful heavens," I sighed. "That was a complete waste of time, was it not? The man is no more than an automaton."

"Do you really think so, Watson?" came the reply. I sighed inwardly and knew better than respond.

Chapter Five

Over a Pint at The Eagle

We made our way out of the building and on to Bene't Street where we stood in the cool summer afternoon.

"Very well, Holmes. Where to now?"

"About twenty paces to the left."

"Please, Holmes. A straightforward answer would be just fine."

"Fine then. After that, cross the road."

I looked in the direction he was indicating, and my eye came to rest on the entrance to *The Eagle Public House*. Not a bad idea, a pint at the end of the afternoon. Would not mind that at all.

"Victor Hatherley should be waiting for us inside," added Holmes.

A sign above the door said that the pub had been serving students and fellows since 1799. It was a dark but cheerful place inside and was not yet crowded with punters and carousers celebrating the end of classes for the day. At a table by the back wall sat Victor Hatherley. He rose to greet us, and I was pleased to see that the crutches had been discarded, and he was now using only a cane. His sprain would be entirely gone within a week.

"Ah, Victor," said Holmes as we met. "We have spent an excellent day with your colleagues …"

He said no more as the young man interrupted him.

"It happened just as you said it would Mr. Holmes. Look. This letter appeared in my box this afternoon." He held out an opened envelope as he spoke. Holmes took it and sat down. Before opening it, he lit up his pipe and called the barmaid over to the table and ordered a round of ale. Poor Victor seemed ready to leap out of his chair, take Holmes by the lapels and force him to start reading.

Holmes took several drafts on his pipe, and a long sip of his ale and then opened the letter. He read it and nodded and then handed it over to me. It ran:

Your mother is our prisoner. She is alive and being well-treated. If you ever wish to see her again, you must provide us with the information we need concerning the Admiralty project, and she will be returned to you safely. If you do not, you will find your mother at the bottom of the Thames.

Within twenty-four hours, you must confirm that you are willing to cooperate with us. Leave an envelope addressed to yourself under the trash bin in the arch of the first window to the left of the front door of the train station.

Any contact with the police will result in the immediate and painful death of your mother.

"Do you really think they would hurt her?" asked the distraught young man.

"No," replied Holmes. "I think not. The threat of hurting her is infinitely more powerful than the actual act. From what you have said of her, I suspect that any physical pain inflicted is more likely to be administered by your mother upon her captors than the reverse."

Victor gave a forced smile. "I am sure you are right, sir. But I cannot sleep, and I cannot stop worrying. So please, sir, what must happen next? Can we get at the task immediately?"

"Most certainly," came the reply from Holmes. "We may get started. As I told you yesterday, it will be necessary for us to draw out the process and, in doing so, give these criminals sufficient opportunity to give themselves away. That does not negate having you begin now to write an anguished, desperate letter, full of passion and irrational emotional outbursts calling these chaps every nasty name you can think of and demanding irrefutable proof that your mother is still alive. Otherwise, you will have come to the conclusion that these blackguards have done her in. So, very well, young man, start writing."

Holmes's instructions were met with a blank look, bordering on bewildered helplessness from the young scientist.

"Sir," he pleaded. "What you are asking me is impossible. I am a scientist, not a writer of sensational pot-boilers. I only know how to write with precision and concision, and my writing is totally and deliberately void of everything you are demanding. I simply do not know how to write that way."

"Fret not," said Holmes. "Dr. Watson does, and he is exceptionally successful in doing so. The two of you can draft out your letter while I focus my thoughts with a pipe or two and stroll along the River Cam. I will return in an hour."

Had we been sitting beside the River Cam instead of inside The Eagle, I would have been tempted to give my dear friend a kick right into it. Instead, I merely gagged on my ale and watched him walk out of the pub.

Victor and I went to work, and by the time Holmes had returned, we had what I considered to be a convincing return letter to those who were holding his mom. Holmes read it over and gave his assessment.

"Brilliant. Such a pity, Victor, that you have not learned the secrets of writing sensational drivel. It has the wherewithal to bring in a reliable stream of income. Does it not, Watson?"

I glared back at him but held my tongue. Instead, I offered, "Shall we place it under the trash bin as requested?"

"Heavens no. When dealing with criminals, one must never appear to be too eager. I think that tomorrow around this time would be quite in order."

"But sir," gasped Victor, "they said twenty-four hours or else they would kill her."

"My dear young man, the last thing they want on their hands is a dead mother and no useful information. Let them bite their nails for an hour or two thinking that you have either run to the police or abandoned your mom. Criminals who are on edge are much more entertaining to joust with. So put the letter there after tea time tomorrow and wait until you hear back from them. Advise me as soon as they respond. And now, young scientist, back to your lodgings and get some sleep. There is important work for you to do in your laboratory. I bid you good-day and will await your next contact with me."

Holmes rose. "Come, Watson, this game is on a time-out for a day or two. Back to London."

I put a hand on Victor's shoulder and assured him that following the instructions given to him by Sherlock Holmes was the best course for rescuing his mother. He did not appear to be at all at ease.

On the train, while returning to London, I finally had a chance to tackle Holmes on his comments to me earlier in the day.

"Really Holmes," I began, "you can play cat and mouse with your suspects all you want, but I am not keen on your doing it with me. Now out with it. What in the world did you see in those people that I did not?"

"With whom did you wish me to begin?"

"Oh, for pity sake, start with Professor Lysander Stark. That was his full name was it not?"

"Really? Was that indeed his name?"

I felt a bit confident in responding to that one. "I observed," I said, with some emphasis on my verb, "that his name in his younger years was Ludwig Zimmerman."

"Excellent Watson. There were certificates all over his wall, some in English and some in German. Those in German all bore the name of Ludwig Siegfried Zimmerman."

"A perfectly normal German name," I replied. "Quite a mouthful for a career in England. Quite understandable that he would change it to something more acceptable when he moved to Cambridge."

Holmes tilted his head to the side and gave me a sidewards look. "By the good Saint Andy, Watson, did they not teach you even the basics of the German language up there in Edinburgh?"

I paused and reflected, and then a veil was parted in my memory. "Aha! Zimmerman. Yes. The German name for a carpenter. The same as the family name of Professor Elise Carpenter. So, yes. As Victor said, they could indeed be related to each other."

"And did you happen to notice the family photo in the upper left corner of the wall?"

I confessed that I must have missed that one.

"It showed an older gentleman, *Herr Reinhard Zimmerman,* with a much younger wife and two children. The boy was already a youth, and the girl was still a toddler."

"Yes, keep going, Holmes."

"The boy's name was Ludwig, and the girl was Elise."

"Why, then they are brother and sister."

"Yes, and they are living as husband and wife."

I was speechless. "Merciful heavens," I sputtered. "That would be against the laws of all civilized countries as well as the laws of nature. That is a very serious charge to make, Holmes. I saw no evidence of that at all. Can you prove that?"

"Easily, since unlike you, I was not merely looking while failing to observe. In the first place, both of them had a few short dark hairs attached to the lower parts of their clothing. I managed to pluck one off Professor Carpenter's skirt as she passed. It was a canine hair, from a German Shepherd. Professor Stark had the same type on the legs of his trousers."

"Really Holmes, that proves nothing. If they are both of German heritage, then it is quite possible that they both own that breed of dog. The Germans are all quite fond of them."

"Both his shirt and her blouse had small spots of a dark wine. I have not yet made the same intense study of wine markings as I have of tobacco residue, but I observed that they had the exact same coloring, and I would venture to guess that they both came from a glass of Dornfelder."

"Honestly Holmes. That is even more tenuous than the dog hair. Of course, they would share the same taste in wine, and no one expects anyone from the continent to be as careful not to spill a drop as we do of decent English folk. What next? The same cigarette tobacco?"

"Well done, Watson. Yes. In the ashtray, there were four cigarette stubs, all from the *Cigaretten Laferme Dresden* variety."

"Very well then, the Professor enjoys his favorite tobacco, as do you."

"One of the stubs had a trace of lipstick on it."

"So they both are patriotic to their tobacco as well as wines and dogs."

"Did you not notice that she bore the distinct scent of Farina perfume?"

"No. And you cannot tell me that he was smelling of the same German perfume."

Holmes again gave me a bit of a look and a sly smile. "Yes, my dear Watson, I can. It was faint, but it was unmistakable. Not sufficiently intense to have been applied directly, only to have been acquired in an amorous embrace of one who was wearing it."

I shook my head at what was now a most unsavory conclusion. "If they are indeed brother and sister and living conjugally, then it is indeed a very dark secret that they are hiding."

"I would not leap to that conclusion," said Holmes. "From the family photograph, it would appear that Herr Zimmerman married a young widow after the death of his wife. The children were stepsiblings but with no issue of consanguinity between them. The law is murky on such relationships as there are no genetic reasons for forbidding such marriages, although it is strongly frowned upon."

I thought for a moment. "Do you suspect," I asked, "that that was the reason they were willing to hint at the possibility that he is spying for the German government? To send you down that path and divert you from their true secret?"

"Oh, well done, Watson."

"Of course, they could still be spies."

"Well done again, Watson. You are excelling yourself."

Chapter Six

Cheaters Never Prosper

Four days later, a note came to me from Holmes. It ran:

Received reply from Victor. Please drop by this evening. Your literary skills again may be needed.

Although I was still inwardly fuming over Holmes's opinion of my stories, I could not resist the thrill of the chase and so showed up as requested. He handed me a letter that Victor had expressed from Cambridge. In it was a photograph of an older lady that I assumed was Miss Gertrude Ring, holding the front page of *The Times* from two days earlier, along with a note repeating her captors' demands.

"It looks as though they have complied," I said. "Very well. What happens next?"

"Really Watson, you cannot possibly be willing to roll over that easily. Look at the photograph. The woman's face is blurred. They could have used any lady, and with the appropriate dress and hair made her look like Gertrude Ring. They have not complied adequately at all. At least, that is what you are going to put into writing back to them. Another anguished letter, please sir."

"But who else could it have been? Surely you do not believe that the photograph is of anyone else other than her?"

"Of course, it is her," said Holmes. Then he beamed a smile at the photograph and added, "And the spirited old girl is not cooperating at all. She has deliberately refused to keep still while the picture was being taken. I will wager that she is serving these chaps misery for breakfast. But enough, please sir, a letter. This time demand that she send something in her own handwriting conveying some fact that could only be known and recognized by her son so that he will know that she truly is alive. Yes, I think that will suffice."

I did as requested, deliberately making Victor come across as a bit more controlled and calculating and not merely an emotional mess. Holmes approved, and we dispatched it back to Victor.

Four more days passed, and then another note arrived from Holmes:

Reply received. Victor is delivering in person at six o'clock. Could you kindly join us?

By six o'clock, I was seated in my familiar armchair on one side of the fireplace with Sherlock Holmes seated across from me. There was a knock on the door of 221B Baker Street, and I could hear Mrs. Hudson opening it. Then I heard as our seventeen stairs were ascended in five quick steps and felt quite pleased that my treatment of a sprained ankle had been successful.

Victor Hatherley entered the room. He was huffing and puffing, having run all the way from King's Cross. It was a wise man, I thought to myself, who observed that youth is wasted on the young.

"Victor," exulted Holmes. "Do come in and share your news. We are all attention."

"Sir, I am still waiting for a letter in return for the one I sent. But just before I was set to leave the laboratory this afternoon a most unexpected turn of events took place."

"Ah, do tell," said Holmes.

"I was alone in the laboratory and was closing the door. As I came into the hallway, I heard someone approaching me."

"Mr. Jeremiah Hayling-Kynynmound," suggested Holmes.

Victor looked surprised, and Holmes continued. "And what did master Jerry want?"

"He grabbed my arm and pulled me back into the laboratory and closed the door behind us. And as he did, he said, 'Hey there Plum Face, running off early, are we? Going to try and find Momsy?'"

"I just glared at him and demanded to know what he wanted. He said, 'Your Momsy has been kidnapped, you know. She could very well be killed. Or maybe worse, if the nasty boys who ran off with her are practitioners of the ancient arts of necrophilia.' And he laughed in my face. He said, 'It so happens Vicky, my boy, that I know where she is. And I can help you find her, all safe and sound.'

"I was very vexed with him, and I demanded that he explain himself. He said, 'It wasn't all that hard to track down the old girl. Just a bit of detective work by yours truly. Of course, I have a fee for my services, which I am sure you will be happy to pay.'

"I demanded to know what he was asking and how he expected me to believe him. He replied by saying that he would defer payment until my mother was found and that he would accept my word as an Englishman that I would pay up upon finding her. I said ..."

Holmes interrupted him at this point. "And what was his fee? Something connected to all the notes you have written concerning the engineering behind this project of yours? Is that correct?"

"Well, yes sir. That is exactly what he demanded. How could you have known that?"

"There is not time to explain. Please continue with your account."

"First I responded in anger and called him some rather vile names, and he just laughed and mocked me in return and again insulted my appearance. Then I caught hold of my emotions and tried to cool my blood and told him that, of course, I would part with all my documentation as it was a trifle to me, and I would find other things to investigate and submit next year. So could he please deliver on his boast. Then I told him I would meet with him tomorrow afternoon and hand over my research notes in return for his information on the whereabouts of my mother."

"Ah, well done, Victor," said Holmes. "Let us take this matter from here on. Instead of you meeting with him, it shall be Watson and I, and we shall be able, I am sure, to rescue your mother and protect your diligent research all at the same time."

After some exchange of plans for the morrow, Victor departed.

"How," I asked, "did you know that it would be that arrogant young blue-blood?"

"Oh my goodness, Watson. How could it not have been? His story about living on tobacco and coffee for seventy-two hours was utter rubbish. For twenty years, I have steeled my constitution so that I can focus my mind and concentrate on a case, and even I cannot possibly keep it up for more than sixty. His claim was an obvious lie. Furthermore, I said that there had been several accusations against him. He responded to only one. There have been, in truth, at least a half dozen people come forward and made claims against him, yet every one of them has been withdrawn and apologies issued shortly afterward. When that pattern is repeated so often, then it is a sure sign that someone who has access to significant sums of money is paying it out on a regular basis and believes that he can buy his way to whatever he wants. Young Jerry has spent all of his time sculling up and down the river and has nothing to present this fall to certify the research he is supposed to have done. He knew that Victor Hatherley's integrity could never be bought and so he took advantage of his Achilles's heel and kidnapped his mother. A bit of a desperate ploy, but it might have worked."

"Had not," I said in triumph, "Victor managed to run away and come to Sherlock Holmes."

"Ah, my friend. You do not give yourself credit. This case was one that you brought to me else I would not have been asked to assist and thus could not have solved it so readily."

"And will you fully expose the blighter and have him shamed and sent down?"

Holmes closed his eyes for a minute before responding. "No. I think not. Master Jerry is still a young man with a very bright mind and has the potential to do good if he can be turned, forcibly if necessary, back onto the right track."

"And how will you do that?"

"Why blackmail, of course. I will terrify him into getting out of his silly rowboat and into the library and completing his work properly, and I shall keep up the threat of exposing him until he graduates and is no longer tempted to stray. Yes. That is the course I believe I will pursue. I rather suspect that the indomitable Miss Ring would go along with it."

"I would not be surprised if she does. And when shall we accost young Mr. Hayling-Kynynmound? Do you know his place of residence?"

"No, but we do know where he will be at the start of the midday lunch break, and we shall be waiting for him there tomorrow."

The following morning I again met Holmes at King's Cross Station, and we boarded the train to Cambridge. I complimented him again on his solving the case, and I began to make some notes toward writing it up as a story.

"Really, Watson, must you? It has turned out to be one of the more trivial cases presented to me. I confess I had secretly hoped that the villains had turned out to be German spies and not just an obnoxious young aristocrat who cheats. Nevertheless, justice will be served, and our client shall have his beloved mother returned to him."

He then opened a book and began to read. The book was not related to hydraulic engineering, and I was quite sure I would never again see such a book in his hands.

By late morning, we had arrived in Cambridge and walked all the way past through the grounds, across Parker's Piece and Jesus Green to the far side of the River Cam where the University boathouse is situated. As we were approaching, we saw a young man wearing athletic short pants and shirt lifting a single scull shell out of the boathouse and placing it gingerly into the water.

"That's him," I said. "Should we run to catch him before he sets out?"

"No need," said Holmes. "He is a diligent oarsman even if not a student. He will set his blades carefully into the gates and his feet into the shoes and make all the necessary adjustments before pushing off. There is more than enough time."

As Jerry was kneeling on the dock and setting his oars into place, another man in full street dress came out of the boathouse and knelt down beside him. They appeared to exchange a few words, and then the second fellow drew a revolver out of his pocket. We heard the loud, sharp retort of a shot being fired. Jerry's hands went up in the air. His body toppled backward, first on to the shell, and then off into the water. The assailant stood and ran back around the far end of the boathouse.

Holmes and I exchanged a startled glance and then ran toward the dock. We could see Jerry making slow flailing movements in the water. I sprinted as best I could and tossed off my jacket and jumped into the water. I was no champion swimmer, but the BEF had forced all recruits, even those who only served in the deserts of Afghanistan, to learn to swim and so I was able to pull the lad to the dock where Holmes hoisted him out. I lifted myself up from the water and immediately pulled up the thin shirt, now soaked in blood, and saw a wound in the chest, issuing fearful amounts of blood. I applied direct pressure to the hole in the taut young body and feared the worst. "Hold on, Jerry!" I shouted. "Force yourself to keep breathing."

He was looking up into my eyes, and I could see the terror in his. I felt his chest expand and contract as he desperately attempted to keep air flowing into his lungs. Then I saw his gaze wander away from my face. His eyes began to quiver and roll in their sockets. His breathing became irregular and then, first quietly, and with increasing volume, I heard that horrifying sound that I so clearly remembered from my days caring for dying soldiers – the rattle of death. It continued for some ten seconds and then ceased. His breathing stopped. I checked his pulse, and it had vanished. He was dead.

Several students had gathered around the dock and the now deceased body. There was a quiet and fearful murmur coming from them. One took off his coat and laid it over the body. I was now shivering in my wet clothes, and one of the boys handed me the jacket I had tossed off a few minutes ago. He removed his dry sweater and gave that to me as well. A constable appeared, and then another one. Sherlock Holmes spoke to them.

"My name, gentlemen, is Sherlock Holmes. This young man has been murdered, and the crime is related to a kidnapping in Reading and possible treason. Please contact Inspector Lestrade of Scotland Yard and ask him to come to Cambridge immediately."

One of the policemen hurried off. The other repeatedly told the swelling crowd to back away. We waited for some ten minutes until the police wagon appeared, during which time Sherlock Holmes said nothing. He stood, fixed in place, looking down on the body of Jeremiah Hayling-Kynynmound.

Several constables emerged from the wagon and lifted the lifeless body and placed it inside. Once they had departed, the remaining constable told the crowd to disburse and then spoke to Holmes and me.

"You two appear to be the only witnesses. If Scotland Yard is on their way, I think it best that you give your statements directly to them. They should be here within two hours. We will need you to come to the Parkside Constabulary Station at that time."

I assured him we would. Holmes nodded but did not speak. Once the constable had walked away, he turned to me. He could not mask an intense feeling of pain and sadness.

"My dear friend," he said. "Please get yourself to a hotel and some dry clothes. I need some time to be with my thoughts. Could you please come and fetch me when Lestrade appears. I will be somewhere on the Jesus Green." He turned and walked away from me.

I walked to the closest hotel, booked a room, and arranged for some dry clothes. I restored my body with some tea and nourishment and then walked over to the Constabulary Office. I was told that Lestrade would be arriving shortly, and so went looking for my friend. I found him sitting on a bench at the north side of the Jesus Green, close to the edge of the River Cam. I had expected to find him puffing on his beloved pipe and deep in thought. Instead, I saw him bent over with his head in his hands. I approached him and laid my hand on his shoulder, and gave a bit of a squeeze.

"Come, my friend," I said. "Lestrade is on his way."

He did not reply and did not stand. He placed his hand on top of mine and held it tightly.

"My dear friend," he said quietly, "before today I have looked upon several score of corpses, some recently deceased. However, I have never watched a man die. It is not an easy thing to do. You must have endured it many times during the war. Does it get easier?"

"No. Every time is terrible and terrifying. I have been utterly helpless many times and could do nothing but hold a young man in my arms as he quietly and fearfully bled to death."

"I could have prevented this," Holmes said." Had I not been so cocksure and dismissed the case as nothing more than a despicable instance of cheating by a schoolboy. I failed to see that I was dealing with something much more sinister. I failed this young lad, and his family, and myself."

"As did I," I said, "every time a soldier died that I might have saved had I only arrived ten minutes earlier. There is only one solution to the pain that accompanies those memories, and that is to try not to think about them. With the passing of time, the feelings fade, but they never die."

Holmes nodded and slowly rose, and we walked past Christ's Pieces and on to the Constabulary Office.

Lestrade and two of his assistant inspectors were waiting for us by the time we arrived. One I recognized as Inspector Peter Jones. Holmes considered him a dimwit but had respect for his legendary courage and toughness. The other chap, a newer recruit I assumed, was introduced to us as Inspector Bainbridge. Also, at the table was Victor Hatherley, who had obviously been summoned by Lestrade for this meeting, and a police stenographer.

"So Holmes," began Lestrade, "what's this I hear about you showing up in time to watch a lad get shot, pull him out of the river and watch him die? Fat lot of use you've been today."

Holmes did not respond to the taunt but just nodded and said nothing.

Lestrade continued. "Of course, if you did real police work instead of amateur detective-for-hire, you would know it happens all the time. I've lost count of the men I've had to watch die over the past twenty-five years. The only good thing is that most of them were blackguards who were trying to kill me, so I shot them. Far too many were victims of murderers, and two were my own men. And that, Mr. Sherlock Holmes, is the worst thing that can ever happen to a police inspector. So if you are going to be fighting criminals, you jolly well better get used to it."

Again Holmes did not respond. Lestrade changed his tone and got down to business. "You and your pal were the only witnesses, Holmes, so why don't we start with you giving me your statement. And none of your theories. Just the facts."

Holmes again nodded and, in an impassive voice, gave a complete history of the case to date, beginning with my bringing Victor Hatherley to his office and ending with the death of Jeremiah Hayling-Kynynmound. I was not surprised at his orderly account. His memory was superhuman, and his capacity for ordering data was unparalleled. What I did find amazing was his description of the murderer. He told the details of his height and weight, his hair color, his side-whiskers and mustache, the shape of his nose, and his clothing, right down to his boots. When he finished and before Lestrade could comment, young Hatherley spoke up.

"Gentlemen, if I may, that is exactly one of the men that I came upon in my mother's house. That is the one who came after me with a gun."

"Is that so?" said Lestrade. "Then it would seem that I should not have laughed you out of my office when you came in with your story of your crazy mother's latest adventure. I will keep that in mind for the next time you show up."

He then turned to me. "Right, anything to add to Mr. Holmes's account, Dr. Watson, or is your job only to write up this story and make Holmes look like a hero again?"

Following Holmes's example, I ignored the jibe and said, "I can add nothing to the facts of the case or to my friend's description of the murderer. The only information I can offer is that the gun he used today was a Webley British Bulldog. It has a distinct retort to it, and I heard it save many soldiers' lives when in close fighting."

Peter Jones followed my comment, saying, "Aye. I know the sound. If you've heard it fired enough times, there is no mistaking it. A favorite of both soldiers and criminals it is, aye."

Lestrade then turned to Victor. "Very well then, your turn. You, the brilliant young engineer with a face only a mother could love. Holmes says that Momsy is only the bait and that you are the real prize. What do you have to add?"

Victor reached into his inside jacket pocket and withdrew an envelope and placed it on the table.

"I did as Mr. Holmes had instructed and sent the letter that Dr. Watson and I had prepared. As I left the laboratory this afternoon to come here, this envelope was in my box. I have no idea who put it there, but I assume that you will want to read it. The note signed by my mother is unquestionably from her hand."

Lestrade snatched it off of the table, opened it, and held it up so both he and Jones could read the contents. When they had finished, they both just looked at each other, smirked and tossed the pages back onto the table. I retrieved them and made to hand them to Holmes, but he gestured that I should read them first. There was a sloppily written note on the top and much neater one below it. The top note ran:

Now you know what happens to those who try to thwart us. If you do not want your mother to die in the water as well, you will now do as you were told.

The second note was in a feminine hand and ran:

My dear son:

In response to the demand that I write something in my hand that proves that I am alive, I have selected, and my captors have agreed, a description of my early morning routine as you are the only person on earth who has an intimate knowledge of that subject, having shared the same home with your mother for a decade.

I will describe yesterday morning, the seventh of August. I had, as I often do, slept poorly even though the night was completely silent, and no noise disturbed me. I woke, as I do every day to the sound of the dawn chorus. I looked out of my window over the lawns and copses of trees, and after the sunrise at two minutes past six o'clock, I observed many of the birds that you know are your mother's favorites. These included three different types of Shearwaters - the Cory's, Sooty and Balearic - both the Spotted and Pied Fly-Catcher, the Buff-breasted Sandpiper, and a few of those obnoxious crows with the red beaks and legs.

Having completed my morning quiet time with the birds, I read for the rest of the day in the continuous and undimmed sunlight.

It is my hope and prayer that these words
will assure you that I am alive, and well as
no one else could have possibly written
them.

Your loving Gerty-mommy.

Chapter Seven

Mom Sends Us West

My reaction was, I admit, much the same as that of Lestrade and Jones. The note was a chatty piece from mother to son. It proved that she was alive and well on the previous day but gave no other information that was in any way helpful to us.

I looked over at Holmes as he was reading the same notes. What I saw caused me to stop and catch my breath. The look of desperate despondency and despair that had been on his face had vanished. His eyes had brightened, and I could tell he was biting his lower lip to constrain his facial expression. The forefinger of the hand not holding the notes had been pressed against his thumb hard enough for the flesh under his fingernails to turn white. He finished reading and calmly put the papers back on the table and rose from his seat.

"Gentlemen, if you will excuse me, please. It has been a deeply troublesome day, and I require time to make sense of it all as well as to look into some matters in the library. It is imperative, however, that we meet again tomorrow morning. May I beseech you to join me at The Eagle for a good English breakfast at half-past seven o'clock? I assure you it is of great importance."

He did not wait for an answer but quickly made his way out of the station.

Lestrade looked at me, and I shrugged my shoulders. He then turned to Jones and said, "Holmes is a queer bird if ever these was one, but I've seen him like this before, and I know he is on to something. We will see you, Watson, and you, Hatherley, at The Eagle bright and early tomorrow."

Young Victor tackled me on the sidewalk. "What in the world was that all about?" he demanded.

"I am blind as a mole," I replied. "But Lestrade is totally right. Sherlock Holmes is on to something, and we will find out when he chooses to reveal it to us. All I can tell you is to be there tomorrow morning. And I might ask that if you own a firearm, you should bring it along. Do you have one?"

He looked down at the pavement and spoke in a hushed tone. "I do. Mother made sure I had one and that I knew how to use it. But it is a Webley Bulldog. I am terrified that if I admit to owning it, suspicions could be cast upon me for shooting Jerry."

"Not a chance," I assured him. "I own one too and will have it with me tomorrow as well as my Eley's Number Two. See you tomorrow, Victor. As Holmes would say, the game is afoot."

The hotel had kindly dried out my clothes, and I dressed and dined alone. I saw nothing of Holmes all evening and, in the morning, knocked on his door to find it open. The bed had not been slept in, although there was evidence of his having been in the room briefly to bathe and dress. I left the hotel and came out into yet another miserable cold summer morning and walked to The Eagle. Holmes was already sitting at the table with a sack of books by his side. Lestrade, Jones, and Hatherley soon followed me into the pub.

"Out with it, Holmes," Lestrade demanded. "What are you hiding up your sleeve? None of your games now. Out with it."

Holmes smiled in response. "My dear Inspector Lestrade, we are off to rescue Miss Ring and apprehend some nasty murderers, and, if all goes well, prevent a monstrous and treasonous crime. That is all."

"You know where my mother is?" said Victor.

"Most certainly, I know."

"How is that possible?" Victor said.

"Because she told us, almost to the exact spot. Awfully considerate of the old girl, wouldn't you agree, Inspector?"

Lestrade gave Holmes a raised eyebrow and said, "And just where might that be?"

"Unfortunately, it is a bit of a hike from here," Holmes said. "To be frank, it is a very long hike. I do wish the old girl could have arranged to have been held closer, but she did not oblige us."

"Out with it, Holmes," snapped Lestrade. "Where are we off to?"

"Miss Gertrude Ring is being held captive in Cornwall."

"Cornwall?" exploded Jones. "It's at least six hours from here to Plymouth."

"Oh dear," said Holmes. "Then, we shall have to go to Falmouth instead."

"Madness. That's even farther."

"As I said, I do wish the lady had been a little more considerate, but it can not be avoided. That is where she is."

Lestrade was still glaring at Holmes but said, "Very well then, there is a train leaving for King's Cross in half-an-hour. If we hurry with breakfast, we can catch it."

"You might want to send a wire off to your office," said Holmes, "so that a couple of your stalwart constables can join us. Preferably armed and fleet of foot."

Lestrade did not reply but started to devour his eggs and sausages even more rapidly.

The five of us shared a cabin in the Great Eastern's train back to London. We had hardly pulled out of the Cambridge Station when Lestrade produced Gertrude Ring's note to her son and demanded of Holmes an explanation.

"You are asking us to spend an entire day, Holmes, running right across the south of England. I need something more than your brilliant intuition and imagination to keep me on a train past London.

How do you deduce Falmouth from this chatty little note from Gerty-Mommy?"

Holmes sighed. "Oh very well, inspector. If you insist. Miss Gertrude Ring has not been able to live the life she has by forgetting to keep her wits about her in dangerous situations. She has told us almost to the block where she may be found. All you have to do is look at what she is telling us."

"Really, Holmes," I said. "A little more clarity would not be the end of the world. Obviously, none of us are seeing what you did in the note."

"Do you recall," he asked me, "a day shortly after you and I had met when you took a strip off of me for not knowing the Copernican Theory of the Solar System?"

"Well, of course, I recall it," I said. "I was stunned that any civilized human being living near the end of the nineteenth century should not be aware that the earth traveled around the sun."

"And do you recall my response?"

"You said, and I believe I remember your shocking words exactly, 'What the deuce is it to me?' You believed that your brain, like an attic, had only so much room for furniture, and you only permitted those matters of importance to your work to be stored there, and it mattered not a pennyworth if the earth went around the moon. I believe those were your words."

"Ah, your memory is excellent. And yesterday afternoon, the movements of the solar system, along with other aspects of Nature began to matter. I have spent, in years past, some considerable time in the libraries of Cambridge. Not as a student but as one determined to learn those things, I needed to know to properly implement the science of deduction. So I returned last night to the University Library and sought out one of the ancient librarians, who remembered me a bit fondly, and through until the small hours of this morning together, we deciphered the clues Miss Ring had so generously supplied to us. I may have to forget all this information again by next week, along with the basics of hydraulic engineering, but today it has become important."

"Keep going, Holmes," said Lestrade. "Your babbling on about the sun and the moon is nothing more than your showing off, and I have no patience for it."

"Ah yes," said Holmes. "I confess that at times I may be a bit inclined to that weakness when dealing with my dear friends at the Yard. Very well then, what was the first piece of information Miss Ring imparted to her son? She said that she had 'slept poorly even though the night was completely silent and no noise disturbed me.' Is that correct?"

Lestrade had the note in front of him, looked at it, and confirmed Holmes's assertion.

"I have, as you know, no great knowledge of Nature, but even I know that during the summertime I have to listen to those blasted nightingales chirping and singing all night long. There is not a night goes past without them. So how could it be that she, who is obviously a crack ornithologist, did not hear one? Hmm? That could only happen if she were in a part of England in which there are no nightingales."

"I assume that could only be Cornwall," I offered.

"Precisely," said Holmes.

"I did not know that," I acknowledged.

"Neither did I before yesterday, but Miss Ring did and gave it to us. Then, for her next clue, what did she tell us? She said that the sun rose at just after six o'clock."

"She did, yes."

"A few days ago, Watson, you were up and about to take your morning walk when young Victor appeared at your door. What time was it?"

"It was at five-thirty."

"And had the sun already risen?"

"It had just. It was shimmering across the waters of Little Venice."

"And how could it have already been up in London well before six o'clock and only appearing to Miss Ring after six o'clock? The answer lies in the Copernican Theory of the Solar System, does it not? The farther west you are in England, the later the sun comes over the horizon. The only part of the country in which the sunrise is that far behind London is in the far Southwest. If we were too dull to catch the first clue, she gave it to us again. She could only be somewhere in Cornwall."

"Cornwall is a rather large county," said Lestrade. "Finding one woman there will be like looking for the needle in the haystack."

"Exactly," said Holmes. "And so she has further delineated her whereabouts by the birds she notes. All of them are, with one exception, birds that are found primarily along the coast and not inland. And if that was not enough, she refers to 'those obnoxious crows with the red beaks and legs.' Those were her words, were they not?"

Again Lestrade consulted the note and harrumphed his agreement.

"Now then," said Holmes, "yet again I profess no depth of knowledge concerning England's birds and notwithstanding Our Lord's admonition to 'consider the fowl' I consider watching birds a supreme waste of time. But even I know that crows do not have red beaks and legs. I assume you do as well."

"Enough of playing schoolmaster," said Lestrade. "Get on with it."

"There is only one member of the crow family, I learned last night, who fits this description. That is the Cornish Chough. It is common in much of the Continent but only is ever spotted in one small part of Cornwall, and that is the southernmost part of the country."

"The Lizard," said Lestrade.

"Precisely. By the end of the afternoon, we shall be there and shall find our dear Miss Ring."

Victor involuntarily clapped his hands together and was obviously beaming with pride over his redoubtable mother. I had not the heart to point out to him that he had missed every one of her clues, as had the rest of us.

"Except," said Lestrade, "that there are only five of us, and even if I recruit the local constable, there will be too few to search every house in the village."

"Ah, but how many of them have windows that face out on a wide expanse of lawns and copses of trees. It is not a wealthy village, and the number of manor houses could be counted on the fingers of one hand. I can promise you, gentlemen, that within an hour of arriving at The Lizard, we will have found our engineer's mom."

There was no more to say. Victor put his head back and fell off to sleep. Lestrade, Jones and I each took a book from Holmes's sack and tried to redeem the time by reading. Holmes closed his eyes and retreated into his private world, evidenced only by the occasional moving of his lips as he carried on an argument with himself inside his unique mind.

At King's Cross, we got off and caught a local city train across to Paddington. Three more of Lestrade's men were waiting for us there and joined the long train ride to Falmouth. All of the police officers sat in one cabin, leaving Holmes, Victor and I to ourselves. When we were about a half of an hour out from our destination, Lestrade entered our cabin and sat down.

"Holmes," he began, "I was not born yesterday. You and I know perfectly well that whoever is behind this kidnapping and murder, it is not two thugs from Cornwall. They are acting for someone. Now, who is it?"

Holmes nodded. "You are indeed correct, Inspector. Two days ago, there were five people who could have contracted for the kidnapping and the theft of the plans of the Admiralty project. Today that number has been reduced to three."

"If by that you mean that one of them is dead, then you are stating the obvious," said Lestrade.

"It is obvious now," said Holmes. "It appears that Mr. Hayling-Kynynmound somehow managed to discover what had taken place and who was behind it and was foolishly arrogant enough to think he could use it for his benefit. It is a pity. He had some promise as both a scientist and an athlete. But you have noted correctly, he is dead and therefore stricken from the list."

"Who else did you knock off the roster?" said Lestrade.

"I have learned the hard way that even the most cherubic of women can commit the most vile of crimes, and, for that reason, I had left Miss Fawcett on until last night when I struck her off."

"I never met the woman," said Lestrade. "Why did you eliminate her?"

"Try as I might, I could not imagine a motive," replied Holmes. "Her family is wealthy, enough so that her mother established a new college at Cambridge for women at a cost of thousands of pounds. The circle of women she moves in are all quite a furious group of suffragettes who may be ready to do battle royal with the men sitting in Westminster, but they are nonetheless every bit as furiously loyal to the Queen. The thought of treason could never cross their minds. Miss Fawcett herself quite adores Miss Ring, and I cannot imagine her ever wishing to do her harm, and beyond that, she gives undeniable evidence of being in love with her son."

For the next several seconds, no one spoke. Then Victor looked at Holmes as if he had witnessed the Second Coming. "Sir?" he said in a quivering tone. "Did I hear you correctly?"

"Unless there is something wrong with your ears, then you most certainly did."

"Sir, that is impossible."

"Why? Women are far superior to men in their ability to look beyond the exterior layer and into the far more important matter of a man's character. In addition, to having a good one, you also have a very superior brain, which some equally intelligent women tend to find irresistibly attractive. Her face, her body, and her words, whenever she referred to you, all spoke volumes. You are loved, young man, by more than your mother."

Victor said nothing, and the look on his face said that his mind had moved into that sacred place that is only visited by young men who have fallen in love and are loved in return. I worried that he would not come back in time to be of any use in rescuing his mother.

"So that leaves only three. Two of whom are almost certainly acting in concert with each other."

"The Germans, you mean?" said Lestrade.

"Yes, and rather than speculate before having conclusive data, I suggest we concentrate now on rescuing our engineer's mom, and I suspect that soon afterward, we will be able to determine our villain or villains."

Chapter Eight

Liberation at The Lizard

By mid-afternoon, we had reached Falmouth, the farthest we could travel on the train. We got off and were met, courtesy of Lestrade, with not one but two police wagons and six policemen. The horses, harnesses, and wagons were all gleaming, and the constables were perfectly dressed in pressed uniforms and polished buttons.

"It has been," muttered Lestrade, "a miserable cold summer. There has hardly been a single visitor to the coast since last year. The chaps here are bored to tears, and a visit from the Yard and Mr. Famous Consulting Detective is the biggest thing that's happened. Even the boys who were off duty have shown up just in case we have to call in reinforcements."

To his credit, Lestrade personally said hello and shook the hands of every one of the local constables. Holmes and I did likewise, and then we set off south to The Lizard. The roads were good, and the horses rested, and we made excellent time, pulling into the village administrative and telegraph office an hour later. Holmes hurried inside and returned some fifteen minutes later. He was smiling.

"There are only three manor houses in the village. Two are on the north edge and one by the coast."

"How will you know which one the lady is in?" queried Lestrade.

"Victor will tell us," responded Holmes.

Victor was not listening. He was present in body, but his mind was still in outer space.

"Victor!" snapped Holmes.

"Oh, yes sir. Sorry, sir."

"I said that you will decide for us which house your mother is in."

"Sir, I have no idea. How could I possibly do that?"

"How is that ankle of yours?"

"My ankle? Why it is fine, Mr. Holmes. Better than ever. I've been running every morning."

"Excellent. Then you will walk into each of the houses and in a loud voice call for your mother. If you are met by the maid or the lady of the house, and they are looking at you as if you escaped from Bedlam, then you will say that you are so sorry and leave. On the other hand, if you are met by men with guns and they come running for you, then you will turn and run very quickly down the drive and into the nearest group of trees you can reach. The constables will all be waiting there to arrest the villains, and we shall enter the house and release your mother. Unless, Inspector Lestrade, you can suggest a different plan."

"No. That sounds like the best way to make sure the mother is not put in harm's way. As long as the lad can run, he should be fine. They want him alive, or he is of no use to them. Which house do we start with?"

"I think the one by the coast. Housel House is its name. Built recently and large and isolated enough to hold a captive and her guards and not arouse suspicion from the locals."

Our entourage drove south from the center of the village toward the coast. The stately house sat up on a rise with a magnificent view of the ocean. We circled around it, descended to the water's edge, and climbed up through the trees and bushes until we were directly opposite the front of it. A path led from the property east along the coast, and it was agreed that that would be where the constables would lie in wait.

74

Holmes, Lestrade, Victor and I had crawled up the embankment until we were directly in front of the large veranda and main door.

"Are you ready, Victor?" asked Holmes.

"Yes, sir."

"And no heroics," said Lestrade. "Just get in there and shout for your mom, and if they come after you, then get out of there and over to the copse and laneway as fast as you can. Do you understand that, young man?"

"Yes, sir."

Victor leapt up over the edge of the bank and ran directly into the house. We could hear his shouts of "Mom! Mommm-eeee!"

Immediately we heard a woman's voice shouting back, "Victor!" and then shouting "Victor, get out of here. They have guns."

Victor came bounding out of the front door and descended the veranda stairs in one long leap. Behind him were two tall men, and both were moving quickly. Their guns were drawn, and they were agile runners. Victor slowed his pace until they were almost on top of him and then burst into full speed toward the copse of trees. The men followed him and were immediately swarmed by a host of constables who had them pinned to the ground in a few seconds.

Lestrade let out a small whoop of joy, and we walked into the house.

"Miss Ring!" I shouted. There was no answer.

"Miss Ring! It is safe. Scotland Yard has arrived. Victor is safe. You have no need to hide."

There was still no answer.

I could see a look of worry pass across the faces of both Holmes and Lestrade.

We looked into each of the many rooms. When we entered the gabled bedroom on the second floor, we stopped and froze. Miss Ring was standing in front of us. Behind her with one hand over her mouth and another holding a revolver to her head was the man we had watched yesterday as he put a bullet into Jerry's heart.

"It was very foolish of you to come here," he growled at us. "Now put your guns on the floor and walk back out of the house, or momsy gets a bullet through her head."

I looked at Holmes and Lestrade. They nodded, and we lowered our guns. As we did, the man holding the gun, let out a scream of pain and an oath. Gertrude Ring had sunk her teeth firmly into one of his fingers. But while keeping the barrel of the revolver pointed directly at her, he drew the gun back a few inches and then jammed it violently into her jaw, forcing her to release his bleeding finger.

"Don't be a bunch of pussy cats," came a shout from Miss Ring, whose mouth was now uncovered. "For goodness sake, shoot this blighter."

The villain adjusted his hold on Miss Ring and slid his head until it was almost completely hidden behind hers. We could not risk a shot without fear of her being killed.

"I will give you just three seconds to put the guns on the floor or the lady will die. One …two …"

The three of us did as he had demanded and tossed the guns onto the floor.

"Right, now move away from the door …"

That was as far as he got before he let out another scream of pain, and I could see that Miss Ring's hand had attached itself to his nether region and was inflicting excruciating pain in that part of the anatomy that all men are wise not to allow to be squashed.

He let out another curse and moved to strike her hand away. As he did, the distinct sound of Webley Bulldog exploded in the hall behind me. A bullet screamed past my ear, and the villain who was more concerned for his manhood than his life fell back away from Miss Ring and onto the floor. Lestrade was on him in a second with another gun, a Bulldog, that he had pulled from his pocket.

"Bloody well time you got here," said Miss Ring. "And hello there, Victor. Nice shot. Well done, son. Did they get the other two blighters? Splendid. Then I suggest that we get out of this place. I loathe being kept in the same room for days on end. There's a pub in the village. I am on my way. You may as well join me."

She strolled past the three of us and directly into the arms of her son. They gave each other a quick squeeze and walked out of the house.

"I could go for that," said Lestrade. "But first, I have to get to the telegraph office and tell the boys up in Cambridge to arrest the Germans before they hear about what has happened and make a run for it."

"No, Inspector," said Holmes, "you really mustn't do that."

Lestrade gave a hard look to Holmes. "Listen here, Holmes. I will give you credit for finding the lady, but you do not tell me whether or not I can make an arrest."

"Oh, my dear Inspector. I am not telling you not to make an arrest. I am only telling you not to arrest the wrong criminal. Please have someone go quickly and arrest the accountant."

One of the police wagons took off back to Falmouth with the prisoners and the wounded bloke who had killed Jerry. Holmes and Lestrade headed off to the telegraph office, and the remaining constables, Inspector Jones, Victor, his mom, and I all settled in at the Top House, which claimed to the be most southerly public house in all of England.

After a few pleasantries, Peter Jones turned to Victor. "That was quite that shot you took there, lad. What with a short barrel, nipping in between the heads of the inspector and the doctor and popping one into the blackguard's shoulder. You've had a bit of practice, I'll wager."

Victor looked a bit embarrassed. "My mom made me learn how. Shooting practice fell every week in between Latin and math. I've been a pretty good shot since I was twelve."

At this point, Holmes and Lestrade returned and joined us. I borrowed Lestrade's customary command to Holmes.

"Out with it, Holmes," I said. "No playing games. I would have bet my last farthing on the Germans. Tell me where we all went wrong."

Holmes slowly lit his pipe and took a sustained draft. He followed that with a slow pull on his ale. Then he smiled and spoke.

"I did not for one minute believe the Germans were not spies. After all, we spy on them. So it is to be expected. I asked Mycroft for his file on the Professors Stark and Carpenter. He informed me that not only did the Foreign Office know that they were secretly married to each other, but he confirmed that they were also known to be agents of the Kaiser. They were suspected of sending all sorts of sensitive information back to Berlin. However, they were not for one second suspected of trying to steal the plans for using steam turbines to drive warships."

"That makes no sense, sir," said Victor. "I can assure you that once we put those machines into our battleships, every other boat on the ocean will be outclassed. We will have a tremendous advantage."

"Right you are," said Holmes. "I did not say that they will not *copy* our designs, only that they would not *steal* them. For reasons that are beyond all common sense, our splendid British industries, with the help of our banks and the full support of the Exchequer, look forward to selling them everything they need. Our very own fools believe that England will make wondrous profits from our inventions and that by telling all the other nations of the world not to be nasty and copy us they will all do as they are told. Ha. Within a few months, the Germans will make some superficial changes, perhaps even improvements, and put our turbines into their battleships. England's advantage will then be lost. Professor Stark is already working hand in glove with Parsons and Company to sell turbines for warships all over the world. They will make a fortune. They would have been complete fools to engage in kidnapping and murder when a bill of sale would do the same thing."

"But really, Holmes," I said. "How could you have reasoned that it was the accountant. There was nothing to suggest that he was part of it."

"No, my friend," replied Holmes, "there were, in fact, many things. What was the inscription on the clock on his desk?"

"It read," I said, "'For twenty-five years of loyal service.' He has been working for Charles Parsons for his entire career."

"He has been doing nothing of the sort," Holmes shot back. "Parsons and Company only came into existence a year ago. And next, tell me what was inscribed on his cufflinks."

I racked my brain on that one. "A bit foggy, but I believe they have the initials 'V' and 'M'."

"And you assumed, all of you, that the 'M' stood for his name, Malcolm, and the 'V' must have been his wife or former sweetheart or some such person."

I nodded my agreement. I had glanced at the cufflinks briefly and had only a vague memory of them. Victor was asked for his response, but he was back on Planet Dreamland.

"Men," said Holmes, "do not inscribe initials of themselves and their wives or sweethearts with their Christian name in the second position. We always, for reasons that do not need to be belabored, put our initial in first place, followed by the woman's. Is that not correct, Miss Ring?"

"Always."

"The 'V' and 'M' stood for Venner & Matheson. The firm for whom he worked for twenty-five years and to whom alone he was loyal. That firm has been building steam engines driven by pistons for a hundred years. The move to turbines would leave them so far behind they would soon be bankrupt. Mr. Ferguson was their spy. He regularly sent them all the notes and accounts he could copy, but the actual design, the complex engineering behind the new turbines, the part of the project that truly was secret, was held inside the heads of only a few people, Victor being one of them. He knew of Victor's devotion to his mother, and he hatched the idea of the kidnapping. Whether he expected that the thugs hired by Venner and Matheson would go so far as to commit murder, I cannot say. That is now in Lestrade's hands.

"When I made my visit to the Town's Administrative Office this afternoon, I not only asked where the manor houses were located, I also asked who owned them. Housel House is owned by a Mr. Wallace Matheson. That was all I needed. It had to be where Miss Ring was being held."

Holmes had completed his explanation and took another long draft on his pipe and another pull on his ale.

Inspector Jones and the constables all voiced their congratulations to Holmes and then rose along with Lestrade and excused themselves, leaving just Holmes, Victor, his mom, and me. Victor turned to his mom and said, "Mom, Mr. Holmes here says that Philippa is in love with me. I just can't believe that. Is it really true?"

Gertrude Ring looked directly into the face of her son. "Of course, it's true. She has been smitten with you since the day you began working together. It is written all over her. She loves you for the same reason I do, and it is certainly not for your face. It's for what's behind it."

Did you enjoy this story? Are there ways it could have been improved? Please help the author and future readers of future New Sherlock Holmes Mysteries by posting a review on the site from which you purchased this book. Thanks, and happy sleuthing and deducing.

Dear Sherlockian Reader:

I developed the idea for this story with nothing more creative than finding a word that rhymed with *thumb*. Ergo *Mom*. More than one reader pointed out that in the UK, you have "Mum" not a "Mom" and I apologize for having offended any readers over across the pond. However, although I am a Canadian, about ninety percent of my readers live in the USA, and so I was American spelling in all my stories.

When searching for something significant related to engineering in the late-Victorian period, I came across the account of Charles Parsons. He invented the steam turbine in the 1880s and adapted it to drive naval vessels. Two decades later, several of his powerful steam turbines were installed into the largest, fastest and most heavily gunned battleship that had ever been built. It was named *The Dreadnaught*.

The Germans copied it, and the Dreadnaught Race was underway. Naval warfare was changed forever.

The character of Gertrude Ring is based on and a tribute to the exceptional Gertrude Margaret Bell. Her real-life exploits and adventures surpass anything that could be imagined in a work of fiction. If you are acquainted with any young adventurous women, you might consider giving them a copy of a biography of Gertrude Bell and let it inspire her.

Dr. Thomas Bernardo opened many homes for orphans and destitute children during the late Victorian era, and although some of his practices are now no longer acceptable, he is considered one of England's great humanitarians. In the church in which I grew up, one of the much-admired older men, Mr. Ed Turner, was a "Bernardo Boy" who had been packed up and sent off to Canada. His account of his life was very moving.

Philippa Fawcett was a historical person. She was one of the first women to attend classes at Cambridge University. In 1890, she wrote the Third Mathematical Tripos and scored higher than any man by a wide margin. She was denied the title of Senior Wrangler, however, since that could only be given to a male student. Fortunately, those days are now far in the past.

The Cavendish Laboratory in the New Museum Site of Cambridge University was the site of many incredible scientific discoveries, including the structure of the atom and the splitting of it under the direction of Ernest Rutherford. In 1953, Francis Crick and James Watson (no relation) and a team of other scientists working at Cavendish Laboratory discovered the "double helix" structure of the DNA molecule. According to local legend, they announced this breakthrough to their colleagues in The Eagle Pub.

Nightingales are found throughout England, except in Cornwall. The Cornwall Chough is only seen, and rarely, at The Lizard.

The screening of employees to work in top-secret projects of the British government merely by the phrase "we know his people" will be recognized by many of you as the only security measure applied by MI6 to its most famous recruit from Cambridge – Kim Philby.

And some of you might also have recognized the location in King's Cross Station where Holmes was waiting for Watson.

Hope you enjoyed reading it. All the best.

Warm regards,

Craig

About the Author

In May of 2014 the Sherlock Holmes Society of Canada – better known as The Bootmakers (www.torontobootmakers.com) – announced a contest for a new Sherlock Holmes story. Although he had no experience writing fiction, the author submitted a short Sherlock Holmes mystery and was blessed to be declared one of the winners. Thus inspired, he has continued to write new Sherlock Holmes mysteries since.

He has been writing these stories while living in Toronto, Tokyo, Manhattan, Buenos Aires, Bahrain, and the Okanagan Valley. If you have an inde for a future new Sherlock Holmes Mystery or if you would like to appear as a character in a future story, feel free to contact him at CraigStephenCopland@gmail.com.

New Sherlock Holmes Mysteries
by Craig Stephen Copland

www.SherlockHolmesMystery.com

"Best selling series of new Sherlock Holmes stories. All faithful to The Canon."

This is the first book in the series. Go to my website, start with this one and enjoy MORE SHERLOCK.

Studying Scarlet. Starlet O'Halloran, a fabulous mature woman, who reminds the reader of Scarlet O'Hara (but who, for copyright reasons cannot actually be her) has arrived in London looking for her long-lost husband, Brett (who resembles Rhett Butler, but who, for copyright reasons, cannot actually be him). She enlists the help of Sherlock Holmes. This is an unauthorized parody, inspired by Arthur Conan Doyle's *A Study in Scarlet* and Margaret Mitchell's *Gone with the Wind*.

Six new Sherlock Holmes stories are always free to enjoy. If you have not already read them, go to this site, sign up, download and enjoy. www.SherlockHolmesMystery.com

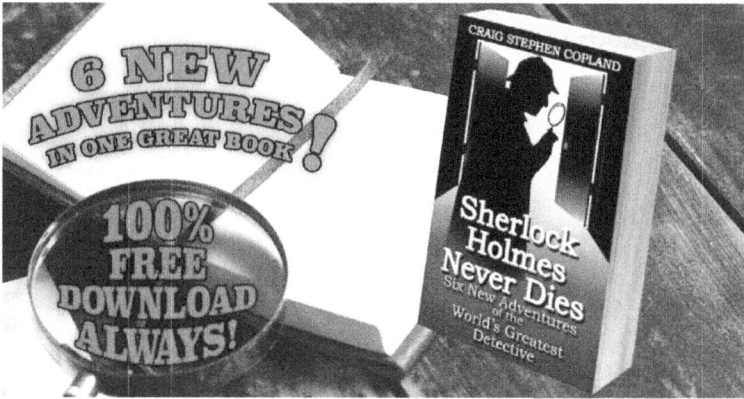

Super Collections A, B and C

57 New Sherlock Holmes Mysteries.

The perfect ebooks for readers who subscribe to Kindle Unlimited

Enter 'Craig Stephen Copland Sherlock Holmes Super Collection' into your Amazon search bar. Enjoy over 2 million words of **MORE SHERLOCK**.

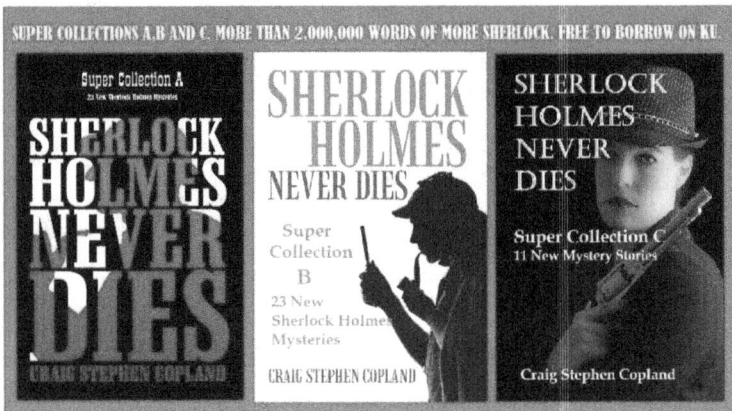
www.SherlockHolmesMystery.com

The Adventure of the Engineer's Thumb

The Original Sherlock Holmes Story

Arthur Conan Doyle

The Adventure
of the Engineer's Thumb

Of all the problems which have been submitted to my friend, Mr. Sherlock Holmes, for solution during the years of our intimacy, there were only two which I was the means of introducing to his notice—that of Mr. Hatherley's thumb, and that of Colonel Warburton's madness. Of these the latter may have afforded a finer field for an acute and original observer, but the other was so strange in its inception and so dramatic in its details that it may be the more worthy of being placed upon record, even if it gave my friend fewer openings for those deductive methods of reasoning by which he achieved such remarkable results. The story has, I believe, been told more than once in the newspapers, but, like all such narratives, its effect is much less striking when set forth *en bloc* in a single half-column of print than when the facts slowly evolve before your own eyes, and the mystery clears gradually away as each new discovery furnishes a step which leads on to the complete truth. At the time the circumstances made a deep impression upon me, and the lapse of two years has hardly served to weaken the effect.

It was in the summer of '89, not long after my marriage, that the events occurred which I am now about to summarise. I had returned to civil practice and had finally abandoned Holmes in his Baker Street rooms, although I continually visited him and occasionally even persuaded him to forgo his Bohemian habits so far as to come and visit us. My practice had steadily increased, and as I happened to live at no very great distance from Paddington Station, I got a few patients from among the officials. One of these, whom I had cured of a painful and lingering disease, was never weary of advertising my virtues and of endeavouring to send me on every sufferer over whom he might have any influence.

One morning, at a little before seven o'clock, I was awakened by the maid tapping at the door to announce that two men had come from Paddington and were waiting in the consulting-room. I dressed hurriedly, for I knew by experience that railway cases were seldom trivial, and hastened downstairs. As I descended, my old ally, the guard, came out of the room and closed the door tightly behind him.

"I've got him here," he whispered, jerking his thumb over his shoulder; "he's all right."

"What is it, then?" I asked, for his manner suggested that it was some strange creature which he had caged up in my room.

"It's a new patient," he whispered. "I thought I'd bring him round myself; then he couldn't slip away. There he is, all safe and sound. I must go now, Doctor; I have my dooties, just the same as you." And off he went, this trusty tout, without even giving me time to thank him.

I entered my consulting-room and found a gentleman seated by the table. He was quietly dressed in a suit of heather tweed with a soft cloth cap which he had laid down upon my books. Round one of his hands he had a handkerchief wrapped, which was mottled all over with bloodstains. He was young, not more than five-and-twenty, I should say, with a strong, masculine face; but he was exceedingly pale and gave me the impression of a man who was suffering from some strong agitation, which it took all his strength of mind to control.

"I am sorry to knock you up so early, Doctor," said he, "but I have had a very serious accident during the night. I came in by train this morning, and on inquiring at Paddington as to where I might find a doctor, a worthy fellow very kindly escorted me here. I gave the maid a card, but I see that she has left it upon the side-table."

I took it up and glanced at it. "Mr. Victor Hatherley, hydraulic engineer, 16A, Victoria Street (3rd floor)." That was the name, style, and abode of my morning visitor. "I regret that I have kept you waiting," said I, sitting down in my library-chair. "You are fresh from a night journey, I understand, which is in itself a monotonous occupation."

"Oh, my night could not be called monotonous," said he, and laughed. He laughed very heartily, with a high, ringing note, leaning back in his chair and shaking his sides. All my medical instincts rose up against that laugh.

"Stop it!" I cried; "pull yourself together!" and I poured out some water from a caraffe.

It was useless, however. He was off in one of those hysterical outbursts which come upon a strong nature when some great crisis is over and gone. Presently he came to himself once more, very weary and pale-looking.

"I have been making a fool of myself," he gasped.

"Not at all. Drink this." I dashed some brandy into the water, and the colour began to come back to his bloodless cheeks.

"That's better!" said he. "And now, Doctor, perhaps you would kindly attend to my thumb, or rather to the place where my thumb used to be."

He unwound the handkerchief and held out his hand. It gave even my hardened nerves a shudder to look at it. There were four protruding fingers and a horrid red, spongy surface where the thumb should have been. It had been hacked or torn right out from the roots.

"Good heavens!" I cried, "this is a terrible injury. It must have bled considerably."

"Yes, it did. I fainted when it was done, and I think that I must have been senseless for a long time. When I came to I found that it was still bleeding, so I tied one end of my handkerchief very tightly round the wrist and braced it up with a twig."

"Excellent! You should have been a surgeon."

"It is a question of hydraulics, you see, and came within my own province."

"This has been done," said I, examining the wound, "by a very heavy and sharp instrument."

"A thing like a cleaver," said he.

"An accident, I presume?"

"By no means."

"What! a murderous attack?"

"Very murderous indeed."

"You horrify me."

I sponged the wound, cleaned it, dressed it, and finally covered it over with cotton wadding and carbolised bandages. He lay back without wincing, though he bit his lip from time to time.

"How is that?" I asked when I had finished.

"Capital! Between your brandy and your bandage, I feel a new man. I was very weak, but I have had a good deal to go through."

"Perhaps you had better not speak of the matter. It is evidently trying to your nerves."

"Oh, no, not now. I shall have to tell my tale to the police; but, between ourselves, if it were not for the convincing evidence of this wound of mine, I should be surprised if they believed my statement, for it is a very extraordinary one, and I have not much in the way of proof with which to back it up; and, even if they believe me, the clues which I can give them are so vague that it is a question whether justice will be done."

"Ha!" cried I, "if it is anything in the nature of a problem which you desire to see solved, I should strongly recommend you to come

92

to my friend, Mr. Sherlock Holmes, before you go to the official police."

"Oh, I have heard of that fellow," answered my visitor, "and I should be very glad if he would take the matter up, though of course I must use the official police as well. Would you give me an introduction to him?"

"I'll do better. I'll take you round to him myself."

"I should be immensely obliged to you."

"We'll call a cab and go together. We shall just be in time to have a little breakfast with him. Do you feel equal to it?"

"Yes; I shall not feel easy until I have told my story."

"Then my servant will call a cab, and I shall be with you in an instant." I rushed upstairs, explained the matter shortly to my wife, and in five minutes was inside a hansom, driving with my new acquaintance to Baker Street.

Sherlock Holmes was, as I expected, lounging about his sitting-room in his dressing-gown, reading the agony column of *The Times* and smoking his before-breakfast pipe, which was composed of all the plugs and dottles left from his smokes of the day before, all carefully dried and collected on the corner of the mantelpiece. He received us in his quietly genial fashion, ordered fresh rashers and eggs, and joined us in a hearty meal. When it was concluded he settled our new acquaintance upon the sofa, placed a pillow beneath his head, and laid a glass of brandy and water within his reach.

"It is easy to see that your experience has been no common one, Mr. Hatherley," said he. "Pray, lie down there and make yourself absolutely at home. Tell us what you can, but stop when you are tired and keep up your strength with a little stimulant."

"Thank you," said my patient, "but I have felt another man since the doctor bandaged me, and I think that your breakfast has completed the cure. I shall take up as little of your valuable time as possible, so I shall start at once upon my peculiar experiences."

Holmes sat in his big armchair with the weary, heavy-lidded expression which veiled his keen and eager nature, while I sat opposite to him, and we listened in silence to the strange story which our visitor detailed to us.

"You must know," said he, "that I am an orphan and a bachelor, residing alone in lodgings in London. By profession I am a hydraulic engineer, and I have had considerable experience of my work during the seven years that I was apprenticed to Venner & Matheson, the well-known firm, of Greenwich. Two years ago, having served my time, and having also come into a fair sum of money through my poor father's death, I determined to start in business for myself and took professional chambers in Victoria Street.

"I suppose that everyone finds his first independent start in business a dreary experience. To me it has been exceptionally so. During two years I have had three consultations and one small job, and that is absolutely all that my profession has brought me. My gross takings amount to £27 10s. Every day, from nine in the morning until four in the afternoon, I waited in my little den, until at last my heart began to sink, and I came to believe that I should never have any practice at all.

"Yesterday, however, just as I was thinking of leaving the office, my clerk entered to say there was a gentleman waiting who wished to see me upon business. He brought up a card, too, with the name of 'Colonel Lysander Stark' engraved upon it. Close at his heels came the colonel himself, a man rather over the middle size, but of an exceeding thinness. I do not think that I have ever seen so thin a man. His whole face sharpened away into nose and chin, and the skin of his cheeks was drawn quite tense over his outstanding bones. Yet this emaciation seemed to be his natural habit, and due to no disease, for his eye was bright, his step brisk, and his bearing assured. He was plainly but neatly dressed, and his age, I should judge, would be nearer forty than thirty.

"'Mr. Hatherley?' said he, with something of a German accent. 'You have been recommended to me, Mr. Hatherley, as being a man who is not only proficient in his profession but is also discreet and capable of preserving a secret.'

"I bowed, feeling as flattered as any young man would at such an address. 'May I ask who it was who gave me so good a character?'

"'Well, perhaps it is better that I should not tell you that just at this moment. I have it from the same source that you are both an orphan and a bachelor and are residing alone in London.'

"'That is quite correct,' I answered; 'but you will excuse me if I say that I cannot see how all this bears upon my professional qualifications. I understand that it was on a professional matter that you wished to speak to me?'

"'Undoubtedly so. But you will find that all I say is really to the point. I have a professional commission for you, but absolute secrecy is quite essential—absolute secrecy, you understand, and of course we may expect that more from a man who is alone than from one who lives in the bosom of his family.'

"'If I promise to keep a secret,' said I, 'you may absolutely depend upon my doing so.'

"He looked very hard at me as I spoke, and it seemed to me that I had never seen so suspicious and questioning an eye.

"'Do you promise, then?' said he at last.

"'Yes, I promise.'

" 'Absolute and complete silence before, during, and after? No reference to the matter at all, either in word or writing?'

"'I have already given you my word.'

"'Very good.' He suddenly sprang up, and darting like lightning across the room he flung open the door. The passage outside was empty.

"'That's all right,' said he, coming back. 'I know that clerks are sometimes curious as to their master's affairs. Now we can talk in safety.' He drew up his chair very close to mine and began to stare at me again with the same questioning and thoughtful look.

"A feeling of repulsion, and of something akin to fear had begun to rise within me at the strange antics of this fleshless man. Even my dread of losing a client could not restrain me from showing my impatience.

"'I beg that you will state your business, sir,' said I; 'my time is of value.' Heaven forgive me for that last sentence, but the words came to my lips.

"'How would fifty guineas for a night's work suit you?' he asked.

"'Most admirably.'

"'I say a night's work, but an hour's would be nearer the mark. I simply want your opinion about a hydraulic stamping machine which has got out of gear. If you show us what is wrong we shall soon set it right ourselves. What do you think of such a commission as that?'

"'The work appears to be light and the pay munificent.'

"'Precisely so. We shall want you to come to-night by the last train.'

"'Where to?'

"'To Eyford, in Berkshire. It is a little place near the borders of Oxfordshire, and within seven miles of Reading. There is a train from Paddington which would bring you there at about 11:15.'

"'Very good.'

"'I shall come down in a carriage to meet you.'

"'There is a drive, then?'

"'Yes, our little place is quite out in the country. It is a good seven miles from Eyford Station.'

"'Then we can hardly get there before midnight. I suppose there would be no chance of a train back. I should be compelled to stop the night.'

"'Yes, we could easily give you a shake-down.'

"'That is very awkward. Could I not come at some more convenient hour?'

"'We have judged it best that you should come late. It is to recompense you for any inconvenience that we are paying to you, a young and unknown man, a fee which would buy an opinion from the very heads of your profession. Still, of course, if you would like to draw out of the business, there is plenty of time to do so.'

"I thought of the fifty guineas, and of how very useful they would be to me. 'Not at all,' said I, 'I shall be very happy to accommodate myself to your wishes. I should like, however, to understand a little more clearly what it is that you wish me to do.'

"'Quite so. It is very natural that the pledge of secrecy which we have exacted from you should have aroused your curiosity. I have no wish to commit you to anything without your having it all laid before you. I suppose that we are absolutely safe from eavesdroppers?'

"'Entirely.'

"'Then the matter stands thus. You are probably aware that fuller's-earth is a valuable product, and that it is only found in one or two places in England?'

"'I have heard so.'

"'Some little time ago I bought a small place—a very small place—within ten miles of Reading. I was fortunate enough to discover that there was a deposit of fuller's-earth in one of my fields. On examining it, however, I found that this deposit was a comparatively small one, and that it formed a link between two very much larger ones upon the right and left—both of them, however, in the grounds of my neighbours. These good people were absolutely ignorant that their land contained that which was quite as valuable as a gold-mine. Naturally, it was to my interest to buy their land before they discovered its true value, but unfortunately I had no capital by which I could do this. I took a few of my friends into the secret, however, and they suggested that we should quietly and secretly work our own little deposit and that in this way we should earn the money which would enable us to buy the neighbouring fields. This we have now been doing for some time, and in order to help us in our operations we erected a hydraulic press. This press, as I have already explained, has got out of order, and we wish your advice upon the subject. We guard our secret very jealously, however, and if it once became known that we had hydraulic engineers coming to our little house, it would soon rouse inquiry, and then, if the facts came out, it would be good-bye to any chance of getting these fields and carrying out our plans. That is why I have made you promise me that you will not tell a human being that you are going to Eyford to-night. I hope that I make it all plain?'

"'I quite follow you,' said I. 'The only point which I could not quite understand was what use you could make of a hydraulic press in excavating fuller's-earth, which, as I understand, is dug out like gravel from a pit.'

"'Ah!' said he carelessly, 'we have our own process. We compress the earth into bricks, so as to remove them without revealing what they are. But that is a mere detail. I have taken you fully into my confidence now, Mr. Hatherley, and I have shown you how I trust you.' He rose as he spoke. 'I shall expect you, then, at Eyford at 11:15.'

"'I shall certainly be there.'

"'And not a word to a soul.' He looked at me with a last long, questioning gaze, and then, pressing my hand in a cold, dank grasp, he hurried from the room.

"Well, when I came to think it all over in cool blood I was very much astonished, as you may both think, at this sudden commission which had been intrusted to me. On the one hand, of course, I was glad, for the fee was at least tenfold what I should have asked had I set a price upon my own services, and it was possible that this order might lead to other ones. On the other hand, the face and manner of my patron had made an unpleasant impression upon me, and I could not think that his explanation of the fuller's-earth was sufficient to explain the necessity for my coming at midnight, and his extreme anxiety lest I should tell anyone of my errand. However, I threw all fears to the winds, ate a hearty supper, drove to Paddington, and started off, having obeyed to the letter the injunction as to holding my tongue.

"At Reading I had to change not only my carriage but my station. However, I was in time for the last train to Eyford, and I reached the little dim-lit station after eleven o'clock. I was the only passenger who got out there, and there was no one upon the platform save a single sleepy porter with a lantern. As I passed out through the wicket gate, however, I found my acquaintance of the morning waiting in the shadow upon the other side. Without a word he grasped my arm and hurried me into a carriage, the door of which was standing open. He drew up the windows on either side, tapped on the wood-work, and away we went as fast as the horse could go."

"One horse?" interjected Holmes.

"Yes, only one."

"Did you observe the colour?"

"Yes, I saw it by the side-lights when I was stepping into the carriage. It was a chestnut."

"Tired-looking or fresh?"

"Oh, fresh and glossy."

"Thank you. I am sorry to have interrupted you. Pray continue your most interesting statement."

"Away we went then, and we drove for at least an hour. Colonel Lysander Stark had said that it was only seven miles, but I should think, from the rate that we seemed to go, and from the time that we took, that it must have been nearer twelve. He sat at my side in silence all the time, and I was aware, more than once when I glanced in his direction, that he was looking at me with great intensity. The country roads seem to be not very good in that part of the world, for we lurched and jolted terribly. I tried to look out of the windows to see something of where we were, but they were made of frosted glass, and I could make out nothing save the occasional bright blur of a passing light. Now and then I hazarded some remark to break the monotony of the journey, but the colonel answered only in monosyllables, and the conversation soon flagged. At last, however, the bumping of the road was exchanged for the crisp smoothness of a gravel-drive, and the carriage came to a stand. Colonel Lysander Stark sprang out, and, as I followed after him, pulled me swiftly into a porch which gaped in front of us. We stepped, as it were, right out of the carriage and into the hall, so that I failed to catch the most fleeting glance of the front of the house. The instant that I had crossed the threshold the door slammed heavily behind us, and I heard faintly the rattle of the wheels as the carriage drove away.

"It was pitch dark inside the house, and the colonel fumbled about looking for matches and muttering under his breath. Suddenly a door opened at the other end of the passage, and a long, golden bar of light shot out in our direction. It grew broader, and a woman appeared with a lamp in her hand, which she held above her head, pushing her face forward and peering at us. I could see that she was pretty, and from the gloss with which the light shone upon her dark dress I knew that it was a rich material. She spoke a few words in a foreign tongue in a tone as though asking a question, and when my companion answered in a gruff monosyllable she gave such a start that the lamp nearly fell from her hand. Colonel Stark went up to her, whispered something in her ear, and then, pushing her back into the room from whence she had come, he walked towards me again with the lamp in his hand.

" 'Perhaps you will have the kindness to wait in this room for a few minutes,' said he, throwing open another door. It was a quiet, little, plainly furnished room, with a round table in the centre, on which several German books were scattered. Colonel Stark laid down the lamp on the top of a harmonium beside the door. 'I shall not keep you waiting an instant,' said he, and vanished into the darkness.

"I glanced at the books upon the table, and in spite of my ignorance of German I could see that two of them were treatises on science, the others being volumes of poetry. Then I walked across to the window, hoping that I might catch some glimpse of the country-side, but an oak shutter, heavily barred, was folded across it. It was a wonderfully silent house. There was an old clock ticking loudly somewhere in the passage, but otherwise everything was deadly still. A vague feeling of uneasiness began to steal over me. Who were these German people, and what were they doing living in this strange, out-of-the-way place? And where was the place? I was ten miles or so from Eyford, that was all I knew, but whether north, south, east, or west I had no idea. For that matter, Reading, and possibly other large towns, were within that radius, so the place might not be so secluded, after all. Yet it was quite certain, from the absolute stillness, that we were in the country. I paced up and down the room, humming a tune under my breath to keep up my spirits and feeling that I was thoroughly earning my fifty-guinea fee.

"Suddenly, without any preliminary sound in the midst of the utter stillness, the door of my room swung slowly open. The woman was standing in the aperture, the darkness of the hall behind her, the yellow light from my lamp beating upon her eager and beautiful face. I could see at a glance that she was sick with fear, and the sight sent a chill to my own heart. She held up one shaking finger to warn me to be silent, and she shot a few whispered words of broken English at me, her eyes glancing back, like those of a frightened horse, into the gloom behind her.

"'I would go,' said she, trying hard, as it seemed to me, to speak calmly; 'I would go. I should not stay here. There is no good for you to do.'

"'But, madam,' said I, 'I have not yet done what I came for. I cannot possibly leave until I have seen the machine.'

"'It is not worth your while to wait,' she went on. 'You can pass through the door; no one hinders.' And then, seeing that I smiled and shook my head, she suddenly threw aside her constraint and made a step forward, with her hands wrung together. 'For the love of Heaven!' she whispered, 'get away from here before it is too late!'

"But I am somewhat headstrong by nature, and the more ready to engage in an affair when there is some obstacle in the way. I thought of my fifty-guinea fee, of my wearisome journey, and of the unpleasant night which seemed to be before me. Was it all to go for nothing? Why should I slink away without having carried out my commission, and without the payment which my due? This woman might, for all I knew, be a monomaniac. With a stout bearing, therefore, though her manner had shaken me more than I cared to confess, I still shook my head and declared my intention of remaining where I was. She was about to renew her entreaties when a door slammed overhead, and the sound of several footsteps was heard upon the stairs. She listened for an instant, threw up her hands with a despairing gesture, and vanished as suddenly and as noiselessly as she had come.

"The newcomers were Colonel Lysander Stark and a short thick man with a chinchilla beard growing out of the creases of his double chin, who was introduced to me as Mr. Ferguson.

"'This is my secretary and manager,' said the colonel. 'By the way, I was under the impression that I left this door shut just now. I fear that you have felt the draught.'

"'On the contrary,' said I, 'I opened the door myself because I felt the room to be a little close.'

"He shot one of his suspicious looks at me. 'Perhaps we had better proceed to business, then,' said he. 'Mr. Ferguson and I will take you up to see the machine.'

"'I had better put my hat on, I suppose.'

"'Oh, no, it is in the house.'

"'What, you dig fuller's-earth in the house?'

"'No, no. This is only where we compress it. But never mind that. All we wish you to do is to examine the machine and to let us know what is wrong with it.'

"We went upstairs together, the colonel first with the lamp, the fat manager and I behind him. It was a labyrinth of an old house, with corridors, passages, narrow winding staircases, and little low doors, the thresholds of which were hollowed out by the generations who had crossed them. There were no carpets and no signs of any furniture above the ground floor, while the plaster was peeling off the walls, and the damp was breaking through in green, unhealthy blotches. I tried to put on as unconcerned an air as possible, but I had not forgotten the warnings of the lady, even though I disregarded them, and I kept a keen eye upon my two companions. Ferguson appeared to be a morose and silent man, but I could see from the little that he said that he was at least a fellow-countryman.

"Colonel Lysander Stark stopped at last before a low door, which he unlocked. Within was a small, square room, in which the three of us could hardly get at one time. Ferguson remained outside, and the colonel ushered me in.

"'We are now,' said he, 'actually within the hydraulic press, and it would be a particularly unpleasant thing for us if anyone were to turn it on. The ceiling of this small chamber is really the end of the descending piston, and it comes down with the force of many tons upon this metal floor. There are small lateral columns of water outside which receive the force, and which transmit and multiply it in the manner which is familiar to you. The machine goes readily enough, but there is some stiffness in the working of it, and it has lost a little of its force. Perhaps you will have the goodness to look it over and to show us how we can set it right.'

"I took the lamp from him, and I examined the machine very thoroughly. It was indeed a gigantic one, and capable of exercising enormous pressure. When I passed outside, however, and pressed down the levers which controlled it, I knew at once by the whishing sound that there was a slight leakage, which allowed a regurgitation of water through one of the side cylinders. An examination showed that one of the india-rubber bands which was round the head of a driving-rod had shrunk so as not quite to fill the socket along which it worked. This was clearly the cause of the loss of power, and I pointed it out to my companions, who followed my remarks very carefully and asked several practical questions as to how they should proceed to set it right. When I had made it clear to them, I returned to the main chamber of the machine and took a good look at it to satisfy my own curiosity. It was obvious at a glance that the story of the fuller's-earth was the merest fabrication, for it would be absurd to suppose that so powerful an engine could be designed for so inadequate a purpose. The walls were of wood, but the floor consisted of a large iron trough, and when I came to examine it I could see a crust of metallic deposit all over it. I had stooped and was scraping at this to see exactly what it was when I heard a muttered exclamation in German and saw the cadaverous face of the colonel looking down at me.

"'What are you doing there?' he asked.

"I felt angry at having been tricked by so elaborate a story as that which he had told me. 'I was admiring your fuller's-earth,' said I; 'I think that I should be better able to advise you as to your machine if I knew what the exact purpose was for which it was used.'

"The instant that I uttered the words I regretted the rashness of my speech. His face set hard, and a baleful light sprang up in his grey eyes.

"'Very well,' said he, 'you shall know all about the machine.' He took a step backward, slammed the little door, and turned the key in the lock. I rushed towards it and pulled at the handle, but it was quite secure, and did not give in the least to my kicks and shoves. 'Hullo!' I yelled. 'Hullo! Colonel! Let me out!'

"And then suddenly in the silence I heard a sound which sent my heart into my mouth. It was the clank of the levers and the swish of the leaking cylinder. He had set the engine at work. The lamp still stood upon the floor where I had placed it when examining the trough. By its light I saw that the black ceiling was coming down upon me, slowly, jerkily, but, as none knew better than myself, with a force which must within a minute grind me to a shapeless pulp. I threw myself, screaming, against the door, and dragged with my nails at the lock. I implored the colonel to let me out, but the remorseless clanking of the levers drowned my cries. The ceiling was only a foot or two above my head, and with my hand upraised I could feel its hard, rough surface. Then it flashed through my mind that the pain of my death would depend very much upon the position in which I met it. If I lay on my face the weight would come upon my spine, and I shuddered to think of that dreadful snap. Easier the other way, perhaps; and yet, had I the nerve to lie and look up at that deadly black shadow wavering down upon me? Already I was unable to stand erect, when my eye caught something which brought a gush of hope back to my heart.

"I have said that though the floor and ceiling were of iron, the walls were of wood. As I gave a last hurried glance around, I saw a thin line of yellow light between two of the boards, which broadened and broadened as a small panel was pushed backward. For an instant

I could hardly believe that here was indeed a door which led away from death. The next instant I threw myself through, and lay half-fainting upon the other side. The panel had closed again behind me, but the crash of the lamp, and a few moments afterwards the clang of the two slabs of metal, told me how narrow had been my escape.

"I was recalled to myself by a frantic plucking at my wrist, and I found myself lying upon the stone floor of a narrow corridor, while a woman bent over me and tugged at me with her left hand, while she held a candle in her right. It was the same good friend whose warning I had so foolishly rejected.

"'Come! come!' she cried breathlessly. 'They will be here in a moment. They will see that you are not there. Oh, do not waste the so-precious time, but come!'

"This time, at least, I did not scorn her advice. I staggered to my feet and ran with her along the corridor and down a winding stair. The latter led to another broad passage, and just as we reached it we heard the sound of running feet and the shouting of two voices, one answering the other from the floor on which we were and from the one beneath. My guide stopped and looked about her like one who is at her wit's end. Then she threw open a door which led into a bedroom, through the window of which the moon was shining brightly.

"'It is your only chance,' said she. 'It is high, but it may be that you can jump it.'

"As she spoke a light sprang into view at the further end of the passage, and I saw the lean figure of Colonel Lysander Stark rushing forward with a lantern in one hand and a weapon like a butcher's cleaver in the other. I rushed across the bedroom, flung open the window, and looked out. How quiet and sweet and wholesome the garden looked in the moonlight, and it could not be more than thirty feet down. I clambered out upon the sill, but I hesitated to jump until I should have heard what passed between my saviour and the ruffian who pursued me. If she were ill-used, then at any risks I was determined to go back to her assistance. The thought had hardly flashed through my mind before he was at the door, pushing his way past her; but she threw her arms round him and tried to hold him back.

"'Fritz! Fritz!' she cried in English, 'remember your promise after the last time. You said it should not be again. He will be silent! Oh, he will be silent!'

"'You are mad,   !' he shouted, struggling to break away from her. 'You will be the ruin of us. He has seen too much. Let me pass, I say!' He dashed her to one side, and, rushing to the window, cut at me with his heavy weapon. I had let myself go, and was hanging by the hands to the sill, when his blow fell. I was conscious of a dull pain, my grip loosened, and I fell into the garden below.

"I was shaken but not hurt by the fall; so I picked myself up and rushed off among the bushes as hard as I could run, for I understood that I was far from being out of danger yet. Suddenly, however, as I ran, a deadly dizziness and sickness came over me. I glanced down at my hand, which was throbbing painfully, and then, for the first time, saw that my thumb had been cut off and that the blood was pouring from my wound. I endeavoured to tie my handkerchief round it, but there came a sudden buzzing in my ears, and next moment I fell in a dead faint among the rose-bushes.

"How long I remained unconscious I cannot tell. It must have been a very long time, for the moon had sunk, and a bright morning was breaking when I came to myself. My clothes were all sodden with dew, and my coat-sleeve was drenched with blood from my wounded thumb. The smarting of it recalled in an instant all the particulars of my night's adventure, and I sprang to my feet with the feeling that I might hardly yet be safe from my pursuers. But to my astonishment, when I came to look round me, neither house nor garden were to be seen. I had been lying in an angle of the hedge close by the highroad, and just a little lower down was a long building, which proved, upon my approaching it, to be the very station at which I had arrived upon the previous night. Were it not for the ugly wound upon my hand, all that had passed during those dreadful hours might have been an evil dream.

"Half dazed, I went into the station and asked about the morning train. There would be one to Reading in less than an hour. The same porter was on duty, I found, as had been there when I arrived. I inquired of him whether he had ever heard of Colonel Lysander Stark. The name was strange to him. Had he observed a carriage the night before waiting for me? No, he had not. Was there a police-station anywhere near? There was one about three miles off.

"It was too far for me to go, weak and ill as I was. I determined to wait until I got back to town before telling my story to the police. It was a little past six when I arrived, so I went first to have my wound dressed, and then the doctor was kind enough to bring me along here. I put the case into your hands and shall do exactly what you advise."

We both sat in silence for some little time after listening to this extraordinary narrative. Then Sherlock Holmes pulled down from the shelf one of the ponderous commonplace books in which he placed his cuttings.

"Here is an advertisement which will interest you," said he. "It appeared in all the papers about a year ago. Listen to this: 'Lost, on the 9th inst., Mr. Jeremiah Hayling, aged twenty-six, a hydraulic engineer. Left his lodgings at ten o'clock at night, and has not been heard of since. Was dressed in,' etc., etc. Ha! That represents the last time that the colonel needed to have his machine overhauled, I fancy."

"Good heavens!" cried my patient. "Then that explains what the girl said."

"Undoubtedly. It is quite clear that the colonel was a cool and desperate man, who was absolutely determined that nothing should stand in the way of his little game, like those out-and-out pirates who will leave no survivor from a captured ship. Well, every moment now is precious, so if you feel equal to it we shall go down to Scotland Yard at once as a preliminary to starting for Eyford."

Some three hours or so afterwards we were all in the train together, bound from Reading to the little Berkshire village. There were Sherlock Holmes, the hydraulic engineer, Inspector Bradstreet, of Scotland Yard, a plain-clothes man, and myself. Bradstreet had spread an ordnance map of the county out upon the seat and was busy with his compasses drawing a circle with Eyford for its centre.

"There you are," said he. "That circle is drawn at a radius of ten miles from the village. The place we want must be somewhere near that line. You said ten miles, I think, sir."

"It was an hour's good drive."

"And you think that they brought you back all that way when you were unconscious?"

"They must have done so. I have a confused memory, too, of having been lifted and conveyed somewhere."

"What I cannot understand," said I, "is why they should have spared you when they found you lying fainting in the garden. Perhaps the villain was softened by the woman's entreaties."

"I hardly think that likely. I never saw a more inexorable face in my life."

"Oh, we shall soon clear up all that," said Bradstreet. "Well, I have drawn my circle, and I only wish I knew at what point upon it the folk that we are in search of are to be found."

"I think I could lay my finger on it," said Holmes quietly.

"Really, now!" cried the inspector, "you have formed your opinion! Come, now, we shall see who agrees with you. I say it is south, for the country is more deserted there."

"And I say east," said my patient.

"I am for west," remarked the plain-clothes man. "There are several quiet little villages up there."

"And I am for north," said I, "because there are no hills there, and our friend says that he did not notice the carriage go up any."

"Come," cried the inspector, laughing; "it's a very pretty diversity of opinion. We have boxed the compass among us. Who do you give your casting vote to?"

"You are all wrong."

"But we can't all be."

"Oh, yes, you can. This is my point." He placed his finger in the centre of the circle. "This is where we shall find them."

"But the twelve-mile drive?" gasped Hatherley.

"Six out and six back. Nothing simpler. You say yourself that the horse was fresh and glossy when you got in. How could it be that if it had gone twelve miles over heavy roads?"

"Indeed, it is a likely ruse enough," observed Bradstreet thoughtfully. "Of course there can be no doubt as to the nature of this gang."

"None at all," said Holmes. "They are coiners on a large scale, and have used the machine to form the amalgam which has taken the place of silver."

"We have known for some time that a clever gang was at work," said the inspector. "They have been turning out half-crowns by the thousand. We even traced them as far as Reading, but could get no farther, for they had covered their traces in a way that showed that they were very old hands. But now, thanks to this lucky chance, I think that we have got them right enough."

But the inspector was mistaken, for those criminals were not destined to fall into the hands of justice. As we rolled into Eyford Station we saw a gigantic column of smoke which streamed up from behind a small clump of trees in the neighbourhood and hung like an immense ostrich feather over the landscape.

"A house on fire?" asked Bradstreet as the train steamed off again on its way.

"Yes, sir!" said the station-master.

"When did it break out?"

"I hear that it was during the night, sir, but it has got worse, and the whole place is in a blaze."

"Whose house is it?"

"Dr. Becher's."

"Tell me," broke in the engineer, "is Dr. Becher a German, very thin, with a long, sharp nose?"

The station-master laughed heartily. "No, sir, Dr. Becher is an Englishman, and there isn't a man in the parish who has a better-lined waistcoat. But he has a gentleman staying with him, a patient, as I understand, who is a foreigner, and he looks as if a little good Berkshire beef would do him no harm."

The station-master had not finished his speech before we were all hastening in the direction of the fire. The road topped a low hill, and there was a great widespread whitewashed building in front of us, spouting fire at every chink and window, while in the garden in front three fire-engines were vainly striving to keep the flames under.

"That's it!" cried Hatherley, in intense excitement. "There is the gravel-drive, and there are the rose-bushes where I lay. That second window is the one that I jumped from."

"Well, at least," said Holmes, "you have had your revenge upon them. There can be no question that it was your oil-lamp which, when it was crushed in the press, set fire to the wooden walls, though no doubt they were too excited in the chase after you to observe it at the time. Now keep your eyes open in this crowd for your friends of last night, though I very much fear that they are a good hundred miles off by now."

And Holmes' fears came to be realised, for from that day to this no word has ever been heard either of the beautiful woman, the sinister German, or the morose Englishman. Early that morning a peasant had met a cart containing several people and some very bulky boxes driving rapidly in the direction of Reading, but there all traces of the fugitives disappeared, and even Holmes' ingenuity failed ever to discover the least clue as to their whereabouts.

The firemen had been much perturbed at the strange arrangements which they had found within, and still more so by discovering a newly severed human thumb upon a window-sill of the second floor. About sunset, however, their efforts were at last successful, and they subdued the flames, but not before the roof had fallen in, and the whole place been reduced to such absolute ruin that, save some twisted cylinders and iron piping, not a trace remained of the machinery which had cost our unfortunate acquaintance so dearly. Large masses of nickel and of tin were discovered stored in an out-house, but no coins were to be found, which may have explained the presence of those bulky boxes which have been already referred to.

How our hydraulic engineer had been conveyed from the garden to the spot where he recovered his senses might have remained forever a mystery were it not for the soft mould, which told us a very plain tale. He had evidently been carried down by two persons, one of whom had remarkably small feet and the other unusually large ones. On the whole, it was most probable that the silent Englishman, being less bold or less murderous than his companion, had assisted the woman to bear the unconscious man out of the way of danger.

"Well," said our engineer ruefully as we took our seats to return once more to London, "it has been a pretty business for me! I have lost my thumb and I have lost a fifty-guinea fee, and what have I gained?"

"Experience," said Holmes, laughing. "Indirectly it may be of value, you know; you have only to put it into words to gain the reputation of being excellent company for the remainder of your existence."

Made in United States
North Haven, CT
24 July 2022

21751886R00068